Roanoke River

JONATHAN LOVEJOY

Armageddon Publishing

Cover: *A Calling,* 1890
William Adolphe Bouguereau (1825-1905)

ISBN-10: 0692316558
ISBN-13: 978-0692316559

For every Sarah

Children of Light

There is no rest from pain

Two take hands in a wilderness alone

Both burning

Jonathan Lovejoy

Roanoke River

The House in the Country

And whosoever shall offend one of these little ones that believe in me, it is better for him that a millstone were hanged about his neck, and he were cast into the sea.

Mark 9:42

My name is Sharon Iris. My sister's name was Sarah. A month before she was killed, she was imprisoned and tortured by my mother and father. One evening, she was injured so badly that she died in her sleep.

The writings of Sarah Maria Iris. (1967-1979).

November 4th, [1979]

I found out they both hate me today. [Mom] said I finally got what I deserved. On the way to the hospital, she told me if I said anything they'd whip me again when I got home.

My whole arm really hurts a lot.

I saw them look at each other when we were on the way home. Mom looked like she wanted to laugh.

The whole world is raining.

November 5ᵗʰ

They told me not to light the lamp. But I lit it when it got dark. I didn't know they would smell the smoke. I won't light it again.

Its cold in here every day. I think its cold because of the rain.

Every time Dad gets home from work they leave, and they don't come back until after eleven o'clock. Its so dark and I hear noises all the time. I can't even get to sleep because of it.

She said they really [punished] me because she dreamed I was rebellious. There was blood this time.

I don't know why she calls me a little bastard bitch because its not true. I have a father.

November 6th

They're not going to let me out anymore. The door is locked all the time now.

I get so [afraid] at night. Sometimes I try to wake up because it feels like I'm in a casket.

I can remember my 1st whipping as plain as day. Mom was standing in the doorway watching it. I wanted her to help me, but she just stood there with her arms folded with a calm look on her face.

I can even remember sleeping in the crib. I used to look through the white bars at night, watching Mom and Dad sleep.

If I go ahead and remember the first thing she did, I won't have to think about it anymore. It happened when I was in kindergarten. She warned me that if I wet the bed again she would do it.

Mom tied my hands behind my back, and then she pushed me on the bed and sat on my chest. Then she punched on my [vagina] until I couldn't breathe. It felt like I had been kicked and would never catch my breath again. I'll never forget it, because her blue jeans were scratching me. She thinks I don't remember but I'll never forget. I never even told Sharon about it.

She was lucky she didn't have to come with us when we moved. Everybody always says how mean their sisters are, but Sharon wasn't mean to me. She even took me out to eat before we moved to this terrible place.

Her and Mom yelled at each other all the time. Sometimes she argued with Mom for the way she treated me. She used to call every day, but she doesn't call much anymore. Maybe she got too busy in the 12th grade.

Mom only looked as beautiful as Sharon when she wore makeup. Her hair was never as long and pretty. She had to use hair [color] to make it as blonde as Sharon's. I don't like to look at her picture because it reminds me of too many things. I know if she was here, none of this stuff would have ever happened.

Mom said that Hell would freeze over before she lets me out again.

When Sharon was younger, I saw her get two [whippings] in one night. She didn't even cry when Mom hit her. But then Dad came and hit her so hard that she lost her breath. I know that the switch cut her skin to blood.

I burned the lamp because I was scared. I told them it was so I could do my homework but I was lying. I lit it because I was afraid.

They can't let me go back to school because the teachers might ask about my arm. Maybe its good that this happened. Maybe they'll stop hurting me now.

But I don't think so.

Aunt Janine used to get angry with Dad for whipping us so hard. She told me that he [dislocated] my elbow when I was little, but I don't remember that.

When Mom brought my sandwich in, I asked her if I could have something to drink, and she said "you're lucky to be getting anything you little shit." I'm going to remember her bad words. She goes to church but she curses all the time.

I could smell her perfume.

They must be going out again.

I will refrain from recording my personal feelings about the physician who treated Sarah's broken wrist. My single conversation with her was frustrating, confirming my worst fears, that the suspicion had rung like a bell in her mind the moment she laid eyes on her. Her exact words to me were "Miss Iris, if I opened my mouth every time I fixed a sad child's broken bone..."

She remembered that my mother seemed like a "charming, compassionate woman," and that my father was very "friendly and humble." Their demeanor, she said, eased her mind so much that she could not imagine they would have ever hurt the child.

November 7th

I was lucky last night. I went to sleep before it got dark. I'm glad its raining because it helps me to go to sleep quicker.

I don't feel too good. I feel kind of sick. Even if they gave me breakfast today, I couldn't eat it.

I feel as skinny as a phantom ghost. I want to float in the air and go through the walls and scare Mom and Dad into a heart attack. I have to get my mind away from them. Away from what they are going to do.

This reminds me of when Bridgette told me she was going to beat me up at the bus stop after school. I was nervous all day long. On the bus she tried to get the other kids to hold me in. But I got away and ran home. I told Sharon and she went with me to the bus stop the next morning. She said "which one of you little piss ants was picking on my sister?" She pushed Leanne in the eye, and said "was it you?" And Leanne said "no," like a whining baby. But Bridgette was nowhere in sight. As soon as [my sister] left, [Bridgette] came out from behind a car garage. My heart turned into a block of ice.

When I think about Sharon it makes me sad. I still feel sorry for her.

I miss the days when we use to walk to Aunt Janine's house. Every Friday we walked over there. One Friday, Sharon got mad because Mom made her hang out the laundry right before we left. She just threw the clothes over the clothesline. When we got home that night, she got one of the worse whippings ever.

Mom took her in her bedroom and closed the door. They beat her for such a long time.

Mom laughs at me a lot. She always calls me ugly. She says my hair is the color of mud. She slaps me and hits me all the time. She says it's because I make faces when she tells me to do something. Once, she ran out of the bathroom [undressed] and hit me in the face with her wet cloth. She wasn't even embarrassed.

I can't believe Aunt Janine is Mom's sister. They don't act anything alike. Sharon is lucky to be there. She doesn't have to worry about being punished anymore.

Mom said that God was judging me for being rebellious. She dreamed I was going to be in a wheelchair if I keep making God angry. I try not to be disobedient. I asked [Him] to forgive me for it.

It's lonely in the country. There are hardly any houses out here, and the nights are pitch black. But the stars are brighter here than in the city.

I feel so sick. It feels like I need to throw up, but

they'll

whip

me

worse

if I do

blue sky

clouds

grapes

watermelon

peaches

strawberries,

November 8th

I tried not to get sick yesterday. But it didn't work. I had to use an old t-shirt to clean it up. Mom said, "Did you get sick in here, you fucking pig? I swear, you're going to get it for this." And then Dad said "you can believe it, you nasty little bitch." He never called me a bitch before.

I almost wet myself yesterday. They might have hurt me worse if I did. They only let me go to the bathroom once a day.

Yesterday after dark, they came to the door. I saw the light from the kerosene lamp glowing under it. And I heard Mom say go ahead and take your belt off. I heard the sound of Dad's belt when he took it off. It was a tinkling sound.

They unlocked the door and came in the room. That's when they smelled the [vomit], and told me to go to the bathroom. It took me a long time because I can only use one arm. When I got back the [kerosene] lamp was on my dresser. I could see the reflection in the mirror. It was like two lamps burning.

They were both in the room waiting for me. Mom was waving her hand in front of her nose, and Dad made me tell what I cleaned it up with. He found the old t-shirt in the closet. Mom said "shove it in her face", but Dad tossed it in the hall and closed the door. It was like the hallway wasn't really there. It was like a black hole.

Mom told me to take off my dress. I couldn't make myself look at their faces. I didn't want to see that quiet smile that's always on her face when I'm getting punished. When I got down to my underwear, she said "get them off too. You're going to get it from your neck to your ankles."

Dad said, "get over here and put your hand on this bed." But she said "No. The wall is better." I remember that I hoped they wouldn't hit my [vagina] again.

Mom took the belt from Dad, and started to whip me. I tried not to cry, but I couldn't help it. It felt like acid on my back. After a few hits, she gave the belt to Dad and said "you better not hold back on her, either."

It hurt worse when he hit me. It was like my skin was peeling off. It seemed like I was blinded.

She took the belt back, and started to hit me on the [behind] again. Dad covered up my mouth and held me. I could hear her grunting while she hit me. She hit me so much it felt like it was being burned with an iron.

After a long time, she stopped. Mom said "you might as well save it because you're going to get the same thing tomorrow night, you hard headed piece of shit." And then, they left. She looked very angry.

I hope nobody ever has to feel what that was like. The pain was too much to bear.

I'm going to start hiding [this] in a better place. If Mom saw it, she would hurt me worse than I can imagine. I keep having dreams about her smothering me. If she tells Dad to hold me, I won't be able to move. It will feel like I'm buried in a grave.

If it wasn't raining so hard, I would try to get away tonight. But I would have to jump to the ground, and I can't do that with my arm like this. As soon as my arm heals, I'm going to run away. I could call Sharon from a phone booth, and tell her everything that Mom and Dad have done.

Dad will do anything that she says. He acts like he's afraid of her. She picks on him until he gets so angry that he does crazy things [like in our station wagon a few years ago]. I remember that it was very cold and dark. I was glad that Sharon was in the back seat with me. Mom and Dad had started yelling real loud. I looked over at Sharon and she had a nervous look on her face. Then, Dad got quiet. That's when I got scared because I knew he was getting angrier. Mom laughed a little bit to herself, and then she finally stopped bothering him. Suddenly I heard a click, and the whole world got pitch black. Dad had turned the lights off and left the orange [parking] lights on. Then [he put the car in another gear] and turned the engine off. We were rolling very fast, and there was no sound. Sharon leaned forward and said "Dad turn the lights on," like she was going to cry. Mom said "Dave honey, please turn them on. Please." Mom reached over and touched the back of his head. I saw a gold watch on her arm.

The car was speeding up. The tires were squalling, and then Mom and Sharon were screaming. She was trying to turn the wheel, and then the car went off the side of the road. It felt like something cold was squeezing my heart. I thought we were going off that little bridge and down into the black water and drown. Then the car moved back on the road, and when we crossed the little bridge the car scraped against the rail. The sparks were bluish white outside Sharon's window. She and Mom were screaming louder. When we got to the other side, Dad stopped on the side of the road. Mom took off her seatbelt and slid over and kissed him. He started the car and we drove home.

While Mom was leaning on his shoulder, she started crying a little.

Aunt Janine said Mom was mean when she was a little girl. Mom would sit in her lap when she was little, and claw at [Aunt Janine's] hair and slap her in the face until Grandma had to make her stop.

Linda.

Sarah was a very quiet, well mannered little girl. She listened more than she talked, and had what I considered to be a very sweet and loving personality. She possessed a keen, insightful intelligence, and a wisdom beyond her years. Her personality was such that she did not have to endure the number of whippings and punishments that I did. She was dreadfully afraid of being beaten, and endeavored to obey my parents in all things. But she was a child, therefore imperfect, providing them with ample opportunity to channel their own frustrations through the lash, onto her fair skin, and into her soul.

November 9th

God didn't hear me. I asked Him not to let them hurt me.

I thought I was dreaming when they woke me up. Mom was in her bathrobe and Dad was at the foot of the bed holding my feet. Mom was holding the belt. She hit my [vagina] with the belt buckle so hard that I couldn't scream. It seemed like the dark turned purple when she did it. Mom and Dad looked like shadows.

She said "flip her over." Mom put her knee in my back. She held my arm so I couldn't grab where she hit me.

He pulled my pajamas down and held my legs. Then Mom bit me all over my back and my behind. She kept biting me so hard that I begged her to please stop. All I could think about was that God was going to help me through it. But it hurt so bad it made me think about dying.

Then she sat on my back. She held my arm and spanked me over and over again. I didn't think she would stop. It was pure fire. After a long time, she turned me over and sat on my stomach. Then she spanked me on the front of my thighs. All I could do was beg for God to please help me. It felt like I was going to die.

But I prayed, and I think He heard me this time.

What am I going to do?

I have to take my mind away—

I'm walking with my sister right now. She is in her white button down shirt and faded jeans. I can see the white house in Williamston, on Sycamore Avenue. We're walking down the sidewalk, past the tall shade trees.

We leave our pretty street now. The houses are smaller. There's a field of tall grass, and the old garage building. "Sharon, you're walking too fast."

We [hurry] past the empty building to the dirt road. The railroad tracks run beside it. I put a penny on them once. The train squashed it as flat as a piece of paper. Soon, we cross the tracks. Sharon is holding my hand now.

I see the apartments where some of my friends live. My school is on this road. Edwards Elementary School. I was in the 5th grade there last year. The schoolyard is as big as a football field. Dad used to play softball out here. A road goes around this whole field. There's no traffic.

The trees are smaller on this side of town. They're not as pretty.

The tall metal fence is behind us now. The new path goes through honeysuckle bushes. They smell like summer. We used to pull the little stems out of the white flowers. The drop of liquid tastes sweet.

Now we're in Aunt Janine's neighborhood. Here's the street where Tim's Store is. He's a very nice man.

Sharon and me stop in his little store. It always smells like sawdust. All the men look at her and smile. Its because she's wearing jeans and a tight shirt. It makes her chest look too big.

Sometimes, I'm nervous with Sharon. I'm afraid she is going to get mad at me. But she never does. She hugs me a lot. She has blue eyes and big, soft lips. Mom won't let her become a cheerleader.

I don't know why she is always so nice to me. I asked her one time why she didn't have a boyfriend, and she said "I do." And I said "Who is it?" And she said "Little Sarah Iris." Then she tickled me until I couldn't breathe.

At the counter, we charge everything to Aunt Janine. She tells us to get whatever we want, and we always do.

There's too many big boys hanging around outside. I once heard one of them call Sharon a [bad name]. She stopped and looked at him like she was going to fight. She kept asking him "What did you say?" He tried to act like he was talking about somebody else. Then we just walked away. I was scared because I thought she was going to pick up a rock and hit him.

Greenville Road is close. We don't take the shortcut behind Ms. Askew's house because a big German Shepard named King is back there. He acts like he's going to break the chain every time somebody walks by. Sharon says "I don't want see that dog today."

We're relaxed now. It feels like we're going to our real home.

Sharon kind of forgets about me whenever we come here. I follow her through the clock living room, through the flower wallpaper den to the strawberry kitchen. There's Aunt Janine at the kitchen table with a grocery list. Her hair is short and [dark blonde] like mine. Her skin is like cream. She is glad to see us, but I can tell that Sharon is her favorite.

I know why they're so close. They're both very nice, and they love to talk bad about Mom. Sharon used to live here when she was a little girl, while Mom was a teacher. Aunt Janine doesn't look like Mom's sister.

We climb into her big, white Lincoln car. The houses on her street are small. The yards have pretty green grass. There's more flowers in her yard than anybody else's. There's a strange yellow flower in the middle of the red ones. Sharon says its our name flower. Bees and hummingbirds come around it all the time.

When we drive past the elementary school, I can see the railroad tracks that go near our house. Sharon gets quiet when we pass [Sycamore Avenue].

There's the big clock tower downtown. The water fountain is huge. At night, the colors pour down a crystal waterfall.

Now we're parked in front of the post office. Aunt Janine is crossing the street to pay the bills. Me and Sharon go into the post office. I want to make a joke that her boobs are too big. I can see them bouncing in the reflection in the post office door. I would tell her, but she might get mad at me. Her hair is as golden as the sun.

Soon we drive out of town towards the country. A drawbridge runs over the [Roanoke River], towards the county where Sharon was born.

We're going really fast now. I love these open fields, and the pine trees in the far off woods. The wind is blowing Sharon's long, blonde hair. She has a peaceful expression.

One Friday afternoon, we were getting ready to go to Aunt Janine's. We were about to walk out the door, when we heard Mom's voice call "Shaaaron!" Sharon rolled her eyes and blew a breath.

I didn't know what was going on until I saw Mom standing by two big baskets of clothes in the kitchen.

"Mom, Aunt Janine is waiting for us."

"It will only take a few minutes."

"Mom, you're kidding."

"It won't take long. Sarah will help you."

I knew Mom had done it on purpose. Sharon wiped her eyes like she was crying from pure anger.

We took the wet clothes to the backyard. The clothesline was under the big pecan tree.

"I'm not doing this. It'll take us a whole hour."

"But she'll tell Dad if you don't."

"I don't care," she said. "I'm not doing it. She's only making us do it because Aunt Janine yelled at her about us." Then, she whispered a bad name about Mom.

She threw the clothes over the line as quick as she could. Some of them fell on the ground and got dirty. Mom was in the house laughing loud. Sharon said, "she's just on the phone. Don't worry about it."

So I didn't.

When Aunt Janine took us home that night, we were happy as usual. It seemed like we were glad to be home so we could get a good night's sleep. But as soon as we got inside, I felt something. The house seemed eerie and gloomy.

When we stepped into the den, Mom was on the couch looking right at us. Her face was relaxed. Dad was in Sharon's room.

"Go to your room, Sarah." Mom said. "Sit down, girl. And you're not fooling me with that fake trembling, so you may as well stop it."

She talked to Sharon for a long time. And then she said...

"Now stand up and take your clothes off."

My stomach dropped like I was on a roller coaster. I thought I was going to hear begging, but she didn't say a word. Then they went in her bedroom and closed the door.

I was holding my breath. It was quiet for so long I thought they weren't going to do anything.

Then the belt whacked her skin. It made me jump. They kept whacking her with the belt, but she didn't cry for a long time. But after a lot of hard hits, she screamed to the top of her lungs. It was a scary scream. It sounded deeper. Like her voice came out by itself. It was so loud and strange that it didn't sound like her at all.

When they finished, I jumped in the bed and pretended I was asleep. I heard them moving towards my door. They opened it but thank God they closed it again.

"She had it coming," Mom said.

I've been whipped a lot in the last few months. I know what Sharon felt that day.

I'll bet its raining in Williamston now. She's probably looking out at the rain, and thinking about me.

My mother controlled my father with her sexuality. She was a beautiful woman, with long, dark blonde hair and deep blue eyes. Shapely figures do run in our family, and she wielded hers with quiet, deliberate skill and purpose.

My father was an intelligent man, in possession of mathematics ability and a rational, scientific mind. Not shy in public, exuding friendliness with easy charm and charisma. But he was weak-willed, hot tempered, and physically obsessed with his wife.

This was the thin, dark haired man ensnared by Linda Iris' powerful sensuality. A weapon she hid under a mask of church dignity and good-natured piety. If women do own a spell to cast, then she owned it, and Sarah Iris was a prisoner of it. They were in deep love, and lust for one another.

My sister and I were rendered powerless by their relationship. Her sadism was filtered into and through my father, until they were both willing parties to it. However much a church woman she may have been, she was a classic sexual deviant—an evil intensified by a seething bitterness for her life and a boiling, lustful contempt for her two children.

November 10th

They had a big fight last night. He left the house and I never heard him come back. I heard Mom begging "Dave please come back," but he didn't.

When she came in the room, I thought I was in big trouble. I thought she was mad at me. But she just said, "Come on, we need to give you a bath." I wanted to ask her what was the matter but I didn't want her to get angry.

It was dark in the house except for the kerosene lamp. She led me down the long hall to the upstairs bathroom. She was wearing her robe and I smelled [alcohol]. I didn't even know that she still drank wine.

This was the first bath I got since they put the new lock on the door. Mom took my clothes off, and she put some water in the sink. The water was ice cold.

"You know you have to be punished when you're bad, don't you?"

She put soap on the cloth and started bathing me like I was five years old. She was washing me slow and smooth. When she got to my [behind] she kept doing it for a long time. Then she pushed her finger into my [private] while she kept pushing into my [behind].

"How does your arm feel?"

She was being to nice to me. She bathed me all over and covered me in a towel. When we got back to the room, she took my towel off and told me to get on the bed.

"Just lie still, and I'll make you feel good."

She started rubbing my [private] again with her finger, and she started licking and kissing on my [nipples]. Then she stood up and took her robe off. She wasn't even wearing a bra. She leaned over and rubbed her [breasts] all over my whole body.

Then she knelt down on the floor. She started squeezing her [breasts], and I think she slid her underwear down but I couldn't see. Then she raised my legs open, and she sucked my whole [vagina] in her mouth.

A few seconds later, she started shaking and breathing real hard. Something must have hurt because she yelled very loud.

When she got up she didn't say anything. She just stood up and put her robe on. She didn't even look at me. She just took the lamp and walked out, and I watched her face the whole time. I remember thinking that Mom looked different.

Maybe it was the lamplight.

$\mathcal{W}$hen I first read my sister's account of her molestation, a cold flash of memory wrenched my body, until I felt so nauseated that I nearly vomited. It forced me to confront something I had refused to remember, but the images could not be contained, claiming every inch of me, tormenting me until I was in tears for many days. There were incidents that occurred between my mother and me, that if I were to dwell upon, might cause me to ramble on at a book length's worth of misery. I was 17 when the worst of it happened, perhaps old enough to cope with the emotional trauma it caused.

But my little Sarah was only 12 years old.

November 11

November 11th

```
        S A RAH
          L
          E
          X
        SHARON
          N
          D
        IRIS
          A H
              A
              R
            O   I
      ALEXANDRA
                I
                S
```

Her and Dad went out last night. Mom was dressed up nice.

I thought my punishment would be over because of what Mom did. But nothing has changed. She acted like she didn't even remember it. She was still mean to me. When she let me go to the bathroom, she pushed me and told me to hurry up.

The lights got turned back on today. I can write when it gets dark [outside].

I hear her downstairs right now, laughing with her church friends. Mom has a loud, screaming laughter.

I dreamed about Sharon last night. I dreamed we were with Mom and Dad in a big, beautiful church. Sharon was wearing a pretty white dress. Suddenly she got a strange look on her face like something was wrong.

"Sarah, we have to get out of here."

"Why?"

She didn't answer me. She just took my arm and started pulling me towards the door. Mom tried to grab her but she snatched her arm away.

The church was full of people. They were all standing up, singing and clapping so loud I couldn't hear myself think. Sharon started walking faster, pulling me behind her until we made it out the front door. We ran until we were in the middle of the church yard. When we looked back, it wasn't a pretty brick building anymore with tinted glass. It was a small, broken down shack that was falling to pieces. It reminded me of a graveyard.

I can hear them laughing again. I don't know why they're so happy all the time.

They're always talking about demon spirits. Mom said that once when she was praying in the dark on the floor, a black [bear creature] with green eyes appeared. One of Mom's friends said that a demon was rattling her back screen door, trying to get in the house. They claimed that a woman was possessed by a demon while they were praying over her, and her eyes turned white and she made a voice like a monster, and then vomited all over the floor.

After I dreamed about Sharon, I had a nightmare that Mom was looking at me through a little hole in the wall, and then she started trying to push through, tearing pieces of the wall off. I woke up hollering and it was still dark outside.

I don't think I'm going to have a very good life.

November 12th

They didn't bring me anything to eat. The only thing they gave me was water.

Mom said she was going to give me the worse whipping I ever got tonight because I [wet] the bed. She said that she was going to stripe the blood out of me.

When they come in the room tonight, I'll have to escape. I'll run past them when they open the door. If I make it outside, I can hide until the next day.

Her friends might know about what she's doing. I've heard them talk about beating the blood out of their own kids. They keep saying "spare the rod, spoil the child", and "train a child in the way she should go."

They hurt me more because Sharon is gone. Sometimes her screaming woke me up in the middle of the night.

Sharon would believe me, if I told her about Mom and me.

The [lady] doctor believed their story that I fell off my bike. I was worried that she might ask me if they did it, but she looked like she believed every word they said.

If my back gets injured tonight, I won't be able to walk anymore. Then they'll keep me in here forever.

I can kneel by the door when I hear them coming. Then I'll push through when they come in. I think I can make it.

It's not raining hard now.

Tonight is a good time to run away.

The House on Blunt Street

For it is a shame even to speak of those things which are done of them in secret.

Ephesians 5:12

here is not enough room in this little book, nor is it wholly appropriate, for me to espouse and analyze the negative effects of a strict religious upbringing. But I am compelled to briefly illuminate the entity—the claw that reached across time itself, grabbing hold of my family's spirit, mind and body.

The International Pentecostal Holiness Church—

The crown jewel—the prim, pristine pride of Protestantism. The Bible from beginning to end—filtered through human minds, corrupted by human hands. It is without question, one of the strictest denominations in the world. In many churches I saw, the level of fear and emotional bondage was remarkable.

My mother loved it.

November 14th

My head still hurts, and my face still feels swollen.

I thought I was going to die.

I can't hardly walk. The white part of my eye is bloody.

I shouldn't have run because it just made things worse. If I hadn't run, I probably wouldn't have been hurt so badly.

There are [streaks] of blood all over my nightgown. It even stuck to my back when I took it off this morning. I feel so weak. I need to eat something, but I'm not even hungry. All they give me is that grape drink, but I want to throw up every time I think about drinking it.

I just need to be tough like a prisoner, until this punishment is over. When they let me go back to school, I'll get to [my sister] then. She'll drive up here and get me, then we'll go to the police together.

My head is still sore from where Dad was holding my head between his legs. I was on my hand and knees, and Mom just kept hitting my back with that belt buckle. She was hitting me so hard that it felt like I wanted to cough.

I don't think they'll let me out anymore until it's over. I have to [urinate] in my yellow sand bucket, and pour it out the window.

I'm losing a lot of weight. I can feel my ribs easier. I'm lucky Dad didn't break one of them, but it hurts like its broken. I can't hardly touch it, it's so sore.

My history teacher said that parents chastise children because they love them.

Dad first [became a Christian] two years ago. He was still a teacher. Everybody in town knew him. He used to smoke two packs of cigarettes every day. After he got saved, he stopped. I remember the day he threw the cigarettes out the car window. Sharon was sitting in the front seat, and I was in the back.

I don't like the churches we go to. The services last for three or four hours. Hell and sin and demons are the only things the preacher ever talks about. They scream and jump around too much. Sometimes the noise makes my ears ring.

One time, a big woman started shouting and jumping behind us and knocked Sharon in the back of the head. I waited for her to get mad but she just got a quiet, polite look on her face, like she was thinking "oops" in her mind. She looked like it had scared her a little.

All of these [Pentecostal Holiness] churches are the same. There's too much loud, wild singing. Some of the older women have hair that looks like it has never been cut in 25 years. They all have dresses and skirts that are so long you can hardly see their feet. They all wear long sleeves even in the summer time. They have testifying services, and they talk for way too long, and they always start crying and saying "Thank you Jesus" and waving their hands back and forth. They sing a thousand songs even before the preaching starts. Then they pray for so long I can't even believe it. Sometimes I wonder if God gets tired of listening to those long prayers.

Mom will probably get a bad disease for punishment, or she might get hurt in a car accident. She acts like she didn't do anything wrong.

They all think she is the nicest lady in North Carolina. She's always smiling at everybody, and inviting people over to the house. And they always invite her over to their houses. The church women always tell Mom she looks like a model. I guess she does a little. Sharon told me if one more person said she's "as pretty as her mother" she was going to puke.

I heard her say every one of them is "boiling in lust." She said they were "so full of hypocrisy it was pathetic."

I like Aunt Janine's church better. It's a lot quieter. It looks pretty inside, and it smells like new carpet. There's nice, new wooden benches instead of folding chairs and raggedy old benches that make your back hurt. Her church is in a pretty brick building with stained glass windows. The churches we visit are always in a little wooden shack or in a trailer. A lot of them are in the middle of nowhere. At night, they look scary. In Aunt Janine's church, the women all have on pretty clothes and hats, and they wear a lot of makeup and perfume. Her church reminds me of a funeral. When you first walk in, everybody is always so quiet and serious. They have ushers that are dressed like nurses. They take us to where they want us to sit. I saw the look on Sharon's face the last time we went. I think Sharon believes a lot of things are stupid, but she's too nice to say anything.

We could have had a good family. But she and Mom were like poison. Mom says she was disobedient and evil, and that's why she couldn't stay with us anymore. She says Sharon was just like Aunt Janine and everybody else in Baptist churches, that none of them are real Christians.

We can't watch rated R movies or listen to rock and roll music. Women can't wear pants and makeup, and they aren't allowed to cut their hair. Everybody in the Pentecostal church looks mean. They always look like they're mad about something. After service they are all tired and smiling. I'll bet they're just happy because service is over.

Our church is called Truth Tabernacle Church of the Holy Trinity. It's a small little wooden building that looks like it used to be an old store. There's a cement slab in the parking lot where the gas tanks used to be.

When we drive out there at night, I always get a strange feeling. It's so far out in the country there are no streetlights. Its beside a big [cropfield] and a thick woods. The first time I ever saw it was on a Friday night. It was a clear summer night full of stars. I kept expecting to see a UFO fly over the trees and land in the big field.

The pastor and his wife looked so happy that people like Mom and Dad had come to their church. Nobody else in that whole place looked as good as they did. They all seemed weird and strange.

There were a lot of cars that night. The pastor and his wife were outside shaking hands with people. Mom and Dad's clothes were so nice they looked like they didn't belong there.

Mom had twisted my ear earlier that night, because I said "I'm tired of going to these stupid churches." The Incredible Hulk was on TV, and I wanted to watch it.

The preacher's wife forgot about everybody else when we got there. She took Mom's hand and walked her down to the front. Me and Dad followed behind them. The church smelled like bad breath. Dad had his arm around me as if he liked me and had never whipped me before.

Everybody was looking at her like she was a movie star. It was the same as it was in Williamston. They all wanted to be her best friend.

Linda Iris.

God knows how they would act if they ever saw Sharon.

Pastor Shaw looks like Bozo the Clown. And he laughs all the time. I think he also looks like Larry from The Three Stooges. And he always wears that same burgundy suit coat or that brown one, and his tie looks like a wide piece of fruit stripe gum. His wife wears the same long white dress every time, with a [doily] on her head.

This is the worst church I've ever seen. Its full of green plastic folding chairs and benches that look a hundred years old. The floor is made out of pure cement. The paint on the walls is chipped from the top to the bottom.

Somebody broke in and stole the air conditioner and broke the big window in the pulpit. Now there's a piece of plastic tacked over that window. If it wasn't for that the ~~muskitos~~ mosquitos would eat us alive.

Sometimes they make the older kids go up to the front. They'll make them stand up there for an hour if they have to, until they start speaking in tongues. One time, one of the older boys fell to his knees and was [spitting] all the way to the floor.

That same night, one of the teenage girls was screaming and running around the whole church. Her glasses flew off. She was in back of the church screaming bloody murder while three women were holding her. Mom acted like she cared about the girl and she didn't even know her.

The pastor got on the microphone and said "she's demon possessed, and she fighting the Spirit. Bring her back to the altar."

Three women picked her up and dragged her back while she was kicking and screaming. Then the preacher said "…we're gonna need the prayers of the righteous. We're gonna need the prayer warriors. We're gonna need the holiest among you. Brother and Sister Iris, we're gonna need you tonight."

The other women got the girl on the floor and held her down. Mom knelt down and put holy oil on her forehead while they held her arms and legs.

"Father God, in the name of Jesus we come before you tonight, asking for the power to cast the Devil from this poor soul…"

They kept [commanding] the Devil to come out of the girl but she just kept hollering and trying to get up. But they wouldn't let her up until she started praising God.

She finally did, but it sounded like she was scared to death because all those women were on top of her. It looked like she couldn't breathe. Mom had her knee on one of her arms and was holding her forehead. The other women were speaking in tongues as loud as I ever heard. It sounded like they were speaking another language.

Mom always looks like she's faking, but doesn't even care if they know it. Some of the women watch her when she has her eyes closed.

November 15th

I just turned twelve back in July. They say that twelve is the [age of accountability]. I got saved in church this summer, and then I got baptized. They said that when I'm thirteen, I have to start trying to get filled with the Holy Ghost, or else I won't be saved anymore. The pastor said that there is a special place in Hell for children who die in their sins.

When I got baptized, it was a cloudy summer day. We were at a big pond surrounded by a lot of trees. Giant muskitos were all over the water.

I walked out into the pond and stood beside the preacher. He put his big hand over my face. His hand smelled like cigarettes and shaving cream. He said "in the name of the Father, and of the Son, and of the Holy Ghost." Then he splashed me backwards in that muddy water. Water got under his hand and in my nose. I tried to stand up but it felt like he was trying to drown me.

I remember seeing the [water's surface] over my head, with mosquitos flying around. I must have imagined it.

I had to hide my notebook, because I heard Mom coming in the room. I put it in the top drawer under my panties. I was scared the whole time she was in here. She brought me a sandwich again. I didn't know how hungry I was until I ate it.

They don't just lock the doorknob anymore. Dad put a [deadbolt] lock in. He acted like it was normal while he was doing it. I wanted to ask him could I go [to the bathroom.]

Sometimes I feel very strange. Backwards, sdrawkcaB

STRANJE

STRAINJ

egnarts yrev leef I semitemos

Maybe that demon girl was possessed with fear, and nothing else.

"Her eyes went white when we got her down." [Mom said.] "It was a sex demon. I knew she was a whore when I first saw her."

She said if that girl doesn't get the Holy Ghost soon, the demon was going to come back, and it would be worse next time.

They also talked about the last days before the [Second Coming], when the sun will go dark, and the Moon will turn to blood. I looked out the window at the full moon while we drove away. I've seen the Moon look like blood before. Sometimes it looks rust colored.

Mom said Sharon had a spirit of sex and witchcraft. She said that's why they couldn't control her anymore.

They were wrong about her. She had a bad temper sometimes, but she wasn't a witch. Mom is closer to witchcraft herself. Witches do bad things to children, and she does things to me even if I don't deserve it.

I knocked on the door when she came by and she let me go to the bathroom. I can't believe it. I almost asked her to please let my punishment end today. I tried, but the words wouldn't come.

She must have saw the blood on my pajamas. I know she saw it, and that might be why she didn't say anything mean.

She watches soap operas all day since the lights came back on. And sometimes she talks on the phone for three hours. More and more people keep coming over.

The preacher said that all of the children better start behaving themselves or he might start doing something that he heard about. In some churches, they make the [disobedient] children go stand up front. Then they pray for them, and whip them in front of everybody.

I can picture Aunt Janine and Sharon sitting in their church. I can see it...

Sharon is wearing the pretty green and black dress that Aunt Janine bought for her 16th birthday. Mom said it made her look like a big [breasted] slut. I don't think I ever saw Sharon look so embarrassed. I think she looked very beautiful.

This Sunday, Aunt Janine will be wearing a pretty hat to match her dress. She makes all of her own dresses. They look prettier than everybody else's.

The carpet in Calvary Hill Baptist Church is burgandy, just like the cloth on the money table. They always give everybody a fan and a program. The program is a bad idea because it just makes you sit there and wish they would hurry up and get to the next thing. The choir marches in from the back of the church. They take forever, and they always look dumb. I can picture Sharon standing there looking so pretty, and trying to have a nice look on her face. Her hair is golden yellow.

The piano is playing now. It makes me wish I could play it myself. There's a big rug looking thing on the wall behind the choir. It's a picture of [Christ] praying [in the Garden of Gethsemane].

I had a nightmare about our Jesus picture. I dreamed that the eyes were looking right at me. Then the eyes got mean and scared me so bad I screamed and woke up. Dad said somebody bought that picture from a carnival for them as a present.

Money is very important in Calvary Hill. They make every person circle around and put money on the money table, and then we go back to our seats. There's always piles of coins and paper money. Those deacons look happy when they're counting it. One of them has a small head and neck. He's a grown man and he's as small as a teenager. He smokes a cigarette outside the church every Sunday.

Boys are always trying to talk to Sharon at that [Baptist] church. Sometimes they will stare right at her chest while she's talking to them. She acts like she doesn't notice it but I know she does.

This is my favorite [photograph] of my sister and me. It was the last picture we took together. Aunt Janine couldn't get us to smile. We're standing by the red azaleas, and Sharon's arm is around me. I can see the tall yellow flower in the background. Sharon said it's a "strange and beautiful flower."

She used to ask me to sit in her room with her while she was doing her homework. Mom and Dad never let her go anywhere. I think she was lonely.

I wish I could talk to her with my mind.

Sometimes I

*I*n sorrow I must confess, that there were times when my strength was weakened, and I was glad I was tucked safely away in my room, listening to it happen to her instead of me. But there were other instances when my heart bore the pain of every single blow, and my body trembled under the weight of her pitiful screams. These were the moments when fear tempered my reason, keeping me from running to wherever they were in the house, to grab the belt or stick from my mother or my father's hand.

I cannot accurately relate the number of times I have been bound in my dreams, feeling the weight of my mother's hand over my face, while my father held me motionless as I drifted into death.

Perhaps, guilt will torment me forever.

November 16th

I can't hardly sleep at night anymore. I have bad dreams all the time. Last night, I dreamed she was holding me down under the covers while Dad punched me in the stomach. When I woke up, it didn't even seem like a dream.

My eye is still red. A pool of blood is gathered in the white part. I don't even remember getting hit in the eye.

It hurts to swallow.

I need water.

I can smell the good breakfast she's cooking, but I don't want any. The thought of eating it makes me want to be sick.

But I do want some cool, clear water.

The sand bucket worked. I put my blue sand bucket on the roof and let rain fall into it. It tastes dusty, but at least I can quench my thirst.

I want to tell Sharon what Mom did. I need to tell her. But she's the only one I could ever tell it to.

Footprints in the Snow
[by Sarah Iris]

There is always something to fear, from a knock at the door. There was a knock, when Mrs. Mills learned that her husband was killed. She became so depressed that she abused her daughter Kathy, and her younger daughter Jenny. Over time she grew more evil, until they were suffering almost every day.

One cold January afternoon, Kathy and Jenny were walking home from school. The ground was covered in white. Snowflakes were falling all around them.

"Kathy please. Let's just run away. We'll go live with Aunt Janine."

"Aunt Janine will call the police," Kathy said. "They'll make us come back. And you know what will happen then."

"But I don't have a good feeling Kathy. I'm scared to go home."

The house was dark gray against the white snow. Their mother's blue car was in the yard.

"Kathy, I've never been this scared."

"I told you, nothing's going to happen. Just keep quiet, and she'll leave us alone."

They stepped quietly through the snow, past the winter tree, to the big two story house. They opened the creaky door, and went inside.

The gray sky made the rooms look darker. They were shivering because of the cold. At the top of the stairs, they heard footsteps in the ceiling.

"Kathy!"

Their mother's voice terrified them.

"You and Jenny get up here and help me! Hurry up!"

They thought it was strange for her to be in the attic. Jenny climbed up first, and she climbed in behind her.

Mrs. Mills was standing on the other side of the dark attic, with her hands on her hips. Her face was twisted into an evil frown.

"Help me carry these blankets down," she said. "Get over here."

They walked over to her. She climbed down from the attic.

"Bring them to my room," she said.

When they picked up the blankets, the door springs creaked. Then it was pitch dark.

They were locked inside.

Through the attic window, they saw the gray light grow darker. The big tree looked like a giant skeleton, as if it had died for the winter.

Kathy decided it was time to escape her mother's evil. After midnight, they climbed out the attic window, and jumped down into the snow.

"We need money," Kathy said.

"But we don't have any."

"I have some hidden in my room."

"We can't go back inside. She'll hear us."

"Mom's asleep," she said. "She won't hear us."

They stepped as quietly as mice to the front door. The door creaked while they opened it. Kathy jumped and almost screamed. Their mother was on the sofa in the dark.

"I think she's dead, Jenny."

Blood dripped from her arm onto the floor. Her eyes were open.

"She killed herself," Jenny said.

"But she kept her promise to kill us first. She wanted us to die in the attic."

"Let's call the police," she said.

"We can't."

"Why not?"

"Because they'll put us in foster homes," she said. "They'll split us up, and I want us to stay together. We have to bury her."

Kathy wrapped their mother's body in a blanket. Together, they carried her out into the woods. They dug a deep grave in the cold ground. Afterwards, they covered her with dirt and snow, and went back into the house.

After school the next day, a friend of their mother's came to the front door.

"Is your mother home?"

"Not yet," Kathy said, "and we don't know when she's coming back."

At twilight, a snowstorm began to blow. Jenny tried to make Kathy call the police and tell the truth, but she wouldn't.

That same night, Jenny dreamed about her dead mother. She was walking out of the woods, making footprints in the snow. The dream came every night. Each time, she got closer and closer to the house. In the last dream, Jenny opened her bedroom curtains, and saw her mother at the window.

The next night, Kathy and Jenny heard a very loud knock at the door.

"Kathy, don't answer it."

"It's not Mom, so stop it. Mom is dead."

"It *is* her," Jenny said. "She'll go away if we ignore it. Kathy don't answer it. Please don't."

Jenny began to cry, so Kathy didn't answer the door. But the knocking grew stronger. They held each other tight, and prayed it would go away.

But it boomed and echoed, like it would break into the house. Even Kathy believed that their mother was at the door.

A loud crash made them scream. Then snowy footsteps appeared at the bottom of the stairs.

The house was colder. The winter breeze whispered.

"Let's go see," Kathy said.

"No! It's her!"

"Let's go, Jenny."

They crept slowly down the stairs. The icy wind whistled through the dark house.

"Kathy look! Look!"

The door was smashed to pieces. Snowy footprints were on the floor, to the foot of the stairs. But when Jenny and Kathy looked outside, there were no footprints in the snow.

"You were right, Jenny. She did come back."

When Kathy called the police, they believed her story, and found their mother's body. Kathy and Jenny went to live with their Aunt Janine, who loved them, and helped them to be happy.

The End

*W*hen the words of a child are presented, there is too much temptation to infuse them with the writer's own polished ability, inevitably hurting, rather than helping the cause at hand. But the more I read her own words, the more I became convinced that she was telling our story better than I ever could. My extraneous embellishments, all the two dollar words and ten dollar phrases began to obscure her clear, easy prose with my pretentious prattle. But even in their purest simplicity, the words themselves are perhaps still astonishing, considering they were all written in the space of a single month, by a girl who had only just seen her twelfth year. And perhaps even more remarkable is that she had never before displayed an interest in writing of any kind.

I am still coming to terms with the idea that Sarah had an insight beyond anything I had ever suspected—especially concerning me and how I felt. But sometimes I sought a level of emotional support from her she was not equipped to give. Yes, there were times when I hugged her too much. There were times when she wanted to go and play elsewhere, but I would coax her into staying with me. I hope to God she never felt like I was smothering her. Even now, I am realizing that I needed her more than she needed me.

But it warms my heart to know her memories of me brought even the smallest bit of comfort in her time of sorrow. For this, I will always be grateful.

November 17th

Sharon was born on a 17th. Her birthday is in June.

She's an 18 year old woman, and I'll bet she has a boyfriend now. Whoever he is, I know he's too ugly for her. And he probably can't see her much anyway, because she likes to read and do her homework. She'll probably become a teacher.

I heard them arguing again last night. They fight all the time, mostly about the Bible. Mom likes to talk about Hell. And she loves to say that people are going there. She says if you don't live perfectly, you'll go there as soon as you die. She claims that she dreamed Jesus wanted to take her down to Hell and show her what was there. But she got too scared, and started calling for Him to take her back. It was dark, and she smelled [brimstone] and heard women and men screaming. She said she didn't see any fire, but it was still burning hot. Dad says that the fire in Hell burns with a dark flame, and people will be trying to bite their skin off like wild animals because of the horrible pain. He says that only Pentecostals can escape it, and that everybody else is [deceived]. I hope that's not true, because Sharon and Aunt [Janine] aren't Pentecostal. Mom said she wouldn't be caught dead in Aunt [Janine]'s dead church, and that just because she went every Sunday, it still didn't mean anything. She said "[Janine] you're going to Hell just like all the rest of them."

I've never seen Mom and Dad in Aunt [Janine]'s church before. I don't think they would ever go.

The rain reminds me of Aunt Diane's funeral. She and Mom really looked like sisters. But Mom acted like she didn't even know her. It's a good thing we were still in Williamston when she died, or Mom would have never let me go to the funeral. She didn't even let me go to Grandma's funeral.

[Lillian Hines] had Aunt [Janine] first. Then Aunt Diane. Mom is the youngest. Aunt Diane liked Sharon a lot. She kept asking her to come to Chicago for the summer.

Aunt Diane and Mom have a different father than Aunt [Janine]. [Aunt Janine's] hair [used to be black], and she's quiet and nicer acting [than Mom]. She acts more like a mother. Her real name is Rosa Lee, but everybody calls her Janine. She won't let anybody call her Rose.

If I ever see her again, I'm going to ask her to please let me call her Aunt Rose. In my heart, I can't call her Janine anymore.

Aunt Diane was nice, but she was wild. She smoked and drank beer, and she read a lot of paper back [romance] books. I used to wonder how she read them so fast. She laughed a lot, and there was always a long brown cigarette in her hand. Her hair was long and bright blonde and she wore a lot of makeup. Her face was beautiful. She touched me on the nose once, and said "Little girls have powers."

She made me kind of uncomfortable. She probably didn't really like young kids. When she came to visit at Christmastime, there would be twice as many presents under Aunt Rose's tree. And whenever she was around, there were people visiting the house I had never seen before.

Her son Craig was the same age as Sharon. He was always thumping me on the head with his finger. Once, when I was little, he was holding my mouth when I had a cold. I thought I would suffocate until Aunt Rose made him stop.

Craig is spoiled and arrogant. His face reminds me of a clothes catalogue. He walks around with his shirt off all the time. Last Christmas, he touched Sharon on her [breast] and tried to run, and she hit him in his back so hard it sounded like a drum.

I think she had a lot of anger building up inside.

I didn't really know Aunt Diane. Christmas was the last time I ever saw her. We found out in January she died of a heart attack [at only 39 years old]. I heard she knew she was going to die, because she was acting like she was never going to see us again. She could play the piano by ear. Maybe that's why Sharon loves [Mozart]. They inherited it from somebody.

I feel like a skeleton.

For some reason, I wanted to laugh at her funeral. It felt like clown ghosts were tickling me. She didn't even look dead. When I looked back and saw Craig crying, I almost lost it. He looked like he was smiling with his eyes closed.

I asked Mom if Aunt Diane went to Heaven.

She said no.

My arm isn't hurting anymore. I think its healing. I'll be able to go back to school soon. Then I can forget that any of this ever happened. I'm going to get so far behind that I'll never catch up. I think I could have got an A in all my classes this time.

I shouldn't have told Josephine that I liked Marcus. She talks too much. I wonder did her brother really tie firecrackers to a frog and light it?

Josephine is supposed to be a good friend of mine. But why does she betray me? She's always teasing me about my clothes. My clothes don't look that much worse than hers. She calls me poor white trash. I don't ever call her names.

I think she likes Kimberly better than me.

When Sharon was 16, I was in the kitchen with her one day while she was washing dishes. She was talking back to Mom, making smart remarks. Mom came running out of the bathroom in her robe.

She grabbed Sharon by the back of the hair and pulled her head all the way back and said "I will slap the taste out of your mouth. Do you hear me!" Then Mom shoved her head and walked back to the bathroom and slammed the door. Sharon had a mean look on her face. She stopped washing dishes for a second, and just stood there with her head down. I was afraid she might throw the dishes all over the kitchen.

There has always been too much violence in this family.

It's dark outside now. I don't think I can sleep with the light off anymore. But if it blows out, I know they won't give me another one.

I've been in this room for two weeks. A fortnight. They probably lied to my teachers about where I am.

Tonight, some people came over before they left. They were all laughing and talking so loud that they sounded drunk.

She dresses differently when they go out alone. When she wears high heel shoes, she's almost taller than Dad. She still sneaks and wears makeup and high heels, and beautiful [evening] dresses.

Nobody knows that she drinks in private. She might even be an alcalholik.

If I turned this light off, I wouldn't be able to see. Not even a faint glow.

My sister wasn't as nice to me when I was little, but we were still friends. I followed her everywhere. She never hung around with anybody her age. She was always by herself, and she used to read a lot of books.

When Mom would come home from work, Sharon would always run up beside the car and pretend she was pushing it forward. I would get behind it and pretend I was pushing it too. One time, Mom opened the door and got out, and when she closed it Sharon started screaming. We realized that her finger was caught in the door. Mom had to hurry up and unlock the door so she could get her hand out. They had to go to the emergency room and they gave her stitches.

The house on Blunt Street had to be the smallest one in the whole neighborhood. We shared a room together. In the summertime, Mom made us go to bed even before sunset. The sun would be orange when we went to sleep. Sharon always slept with a little rag doll named "Gitchy Lou."

Mom and Dad drank [liquor] a lot in that house. They had small bottles of it all over the place. I think she used to get drunk because sometimes when they would be in their room she wouldn't stop laughing.

Sometimes Dad sat at the kitchen table and typed for hours. As soon as Mom got home, she would change clothes and get in her white Oldsmobile and leave. We don't even have that car anymore. In Dad's old station wagon, we saw a snake on the highway. Dad tried to run over it and slammed on the brakes over and over. The tires squealed so loud it hurt my ears. When we drove away, I could feel the snake under the car. I thought it was going to crawl in under the seat.

Sharon and me were outside all the time then. She saw a garter snake in the bushes. She kept screaming at me to look at it but I didn't see it. We looked for it a long time but never found it.

I used to throw sand in those bushes and listen to the sound it made when it fell through. But I didn't know that a wasp nest was inside. All I can remember is the sand noise, and my face burning from being stung by those red wasps.

Miss Ollie Slade lived next door. She was a nice old lady. Her whole house smelled like bananas. There was a lot of fancy furniture and mirrors. Our own house was prettier then. Mom used to have a lot of pretty decorations.

There were only two other houses on Blunt Street because it was so tiny. A giant tree was at the dead end beside the woods. Sometimes I caught Sharon sneaking in the woods without me. But she never told me to go away. We liked to go down the hidden path in those woods to the small stream. We saw a big turtle there once, with a cracked shell. Sharon said it had been struck by lightning.

After it rained, the water rushed by like a river.

Dad caused our puppy to run away, because he used to hit it all the time, and Mom wouldn't feed it anything but dry dogfood. She gave it a giant plate of pigfeet bones once, and he didn't eat a single one. Months later we saw him all grown up. We knew it was him because his front paws were white.

We wanted another pet but they wouldn't get us one. There was a black and white kitten that used to come to our back door, but it had a red collar, so it belonged to somebody else. We fed it and played with it every day.

One summer afternoon, we were playing with that kitten up on Dad's boat in the back yard. Mom poked her head out the door and told us to come inside and take a bath. We wanted to keep that cat so much we couldn't stand it. Sharon put it in Dad's cooler, so we could get it the next day.

The next morning, Dad called us outside and told us to go look in the cooler. As soon as we stepped outside we could smell it. Dad took us over to the cooler, and there were flies buzzing all around it. He made us open it, and Sharon screamed and covered her mouth.

The cat was laying on its side with its eyes and mouth wide open. All of the fur was wet, and we could see that red collar. We had suffocated it to death.

Dad yelled at us both and made us go back in the house. But I was more afraid because of what we did to the poor cat. Sharon was crying even before we got punished.

We never knew when they were going to punish us. Sometimes, we would get bad whippings for nothing, and sometimes they would let us go.

Once, we were talking outside, and I was telling Sharon that I saw a bird with giant black wings flying over the woods. She said "you're lying," and I said "I swear to God I saw it." Mom heard us, and said she was going to tell Dad to whip us because we said "lying" and "swear." She must have forgot to tell him about it.

But there was another time when Sharon got mad at me when I was playing in her watercolor paints. She screamed "you screwed up my paints you terd!" Mom grabbed her by the neck and shook her until she started crying. She told her to never use the word "screwed" again. Sharon kept asking her why, and Mom spelled out the letters "S-E-X." I still don't know what she was talking about.

Dad had a black motorcycle on Blunt Street. I only remember seeing him ride it one time, and that was with Mom on the back. Aunt Janine always talked about how wild he was, and how once he almost skidded into a train.

Dad wasn't even afraid of mice. I saw him hit one with a shoe, and it ran under a pile of toys in our room. He moved the toys out of the way until he found it, and he picked it up by the tail. It looked like a little gray sock.

He and Mom used to take us to the drive-in with them. There would be dirty movies playing. There was one where two pretty woman were kissing naked together. They used to go to the drive-in a lot.

Dad's family lived deep in the country, where there were no streetlights at nighttime. It was pitch dark. They talked about UFO's so much I started expecting to see one. Mom said she saw one at night over the landfill. A red light, that followed them down the dirt road then stopped in the middle of a field. They said it followed them to their cousin's house and disappeared into the sky.

For a long time I thought I had saw one myself, but now I know it was just a dream. It was a blue light in the sky at dusk, over the house on Blunt Street.

The curses that plague a human life are never without origin. Those that plagued my little sister and me are the fruits of seeds sown a generation ago. Both of my parents were raised under the lash, as time and culture saw fit. And perhaps they came from what can be called broken homes, my mother a child of divorce, my father of abandonment.

Of particular interest is my father's childhood, which saw him raised by someone other than his birthparents. His birthmother had died on a cold November evening while he was being born, and his father gladly gave his condemned, writhing little body to the state of North Carolina. Fate granted him no mercy, dropping him into the rough hands of a stern, old time farming couple named Iris, who never once spared the rod of discipline from his poor back.

It is nearly common knowledge that death had loomed like a spectre over his natural mother. It is known that she was always escaping "accidents" and "illness" that should have killed her long before. The years of torturous abuse she endured from her husband may rival anything that a person has ever experienced, and lived to tell about.

And so my mother and father laboured together by predestination. Feeding off each other. Taking from us the proverbial pound of flesh. Administering with evil flair that bitter cup of poison.

November 18th

She thinks I didn't hear what she said about me. I heard it as plain as day when she put those burned, cold pancakes in here. She said, "I don't know why you insist on giving her anything. The little shit." She curses, drinks and does dirty things in private but she's in church right now singing to God and Jesus.

I've seen pictures of her when she was young. She looks like she dated a lot of boys before she got married. She wasn't even a virgin because her daughter was born seven months after. She was doing it with Dad two months before she got married.

Aunt Rose says that Mom was a lazy mother. Mom left Sharon with her so much that she cried whenever Mom picked her up. And she said I wasn't potty trained until I was four.

When I was a baby, Mom made Sharon heat boiling water to warm a bottle for me, and the water spilled all over Sharon's leg. When they took off her pants, the skin came off with it. Her skin was pink and bubbling, like it was cooking.

But Aunt Rose wasn't perfect either. She always had a boyfriend over to her house. Every one of them was already married. She stopped doing that because one of them died in her house. He drank too much ~~alcalhol~~ alcohol with some medicine.

Mom doesn't have any respect for Aunt Rose. She didn't respect Grandma either. Sometimes they talked so mean to Grandma she would start crying. I think they were glad when she died this summer.

Sometimes, when Mom came home from work, Sharon would jump up and wrap her arms and legs around her. Mom would laugh and bend over so she could get down. She seemed more like a regular mother then. She even baked cupcakes for us to take to school.

She let us go to our friends' houses if we wanted. But there was only one girl's house we ever went to named Robin. Her room looked like a toy store. Sharon liked to go over there because of her brother's comic books. Once, she wouldn't let Sharon go in her brother's room, and she got angry and we left. Sharon used to love Superman.

Superman came out in the theater last Christmas, and Mom and Dad wouldn't let us go see it. The movie we had been waiting for our whole lives, and all we could do was sit and watch the commercials. We should have sneaked to go see it from Aunt Rose's House. But we were scared that if the rapture came while we were in the movie theater, we would be left behind in the Great Tribulation.

They say that the rapture will come when nobody expects it. People all over the world will disappear into thin air, and their clothes will be left wherever they were standing. Airplanes will crash into buildings because some of the pilots will be [raptured]. The rapture could happen right this second—

Sharon tried to tell Mom when she thinks the rapture will happen. She thinks it will happen in a split second when nobody in the whole world will be expecting it. She said that God knows exactly when that will be.

Aunt Rose left her husband because he wouldn't get a job, and he tried to control her by hitting her. She said she picked up a piece of wood and tried to split his skull in two. That was a long time ago.

If Mom and Dad can stay married, anybody can. Even on Blunt Street, they had plenty of trouble. I remember two things that happened in that house.

[1] Mom was laying on the bed in her underwear, with Dad laying on top of her pulling her hair. She was crying and saying "David honey, please stop." I can't remember if she was faking or not. She fakes crying sometimes. She'll act like she's crying and there won't be a single tear in her eye.

The other thing I remember very clearly.

[2] They were all in the kitchen, and I was in the living room reading a Childcraft encyclopedia. Mom and Sharon were at the table, and Dad was at the counter cleaning fish with a knife. They started raising their voices like they were going to argue. I didn't look up because they raised their voices a lot anyway. Then Mom screamed "David nooo!!!" When I looked up, I saw Dad with his hand on her face, pushing her head backward and holding the knife to her throat. Sharon had screamed too, and she was leaning over Mom like she was protecting her. I wasn't scared though, because I knew he wasn't going to hurt her.

Dad was always cleaning fish in that house. He went fishing a lot. He kept little cages made of wire, and they were always full of live crickets or worms.

Somebody he knew drowned on one of those fishing trips. It was an old man that was so stupid that he liked to sit on the edge of the boat when it was moving. He fell overboard, but they got to him before he went under. They grabbed his pants, but they came loose because he was so skinny, and he floated out of them and went under and drowned. They found his skeleton two years later in his sweater stuck to a bush.

Mom and Dad knew everybody in town. Everybody we saw said "Hows your Momma and Daddy?" or "Tell Dave and Linda I said hey." They had friends in those neighborhoods with the big, pretty houses. Those houses looked smaller inside than outside. Some of those people were teachers like Mom and Dad were. Mom acted very friendly and happy around her rich friends.

Aunt Rose said that Mom liked to put on airs.

We spent so much time in those neighborhoods that it felt like we were going to move there. Every time we drove down those streets, I got a nervous feeling in my stomach. It seemed impossible for anyone to be lucky enough to get a house there.

They all had big garages and nice cars and trucks. There was a basketball goal in everybody's driveway. The lawns were big and green, and all the trees were set up just right. I used to watch their best friends, to see how they would act when we came over. Mrs. Eva Bailey was Mom's best friend. She didn't have any children. We always went straight to her basement to play pool and pinball. They had a big swimming pool in their back yard that was always pretty and clear. Sometimes we played at a park near their house. It had a small duck pond. Sharon didn't like to go to the park when there were a lot of kids.

Sometimes we stayed at that house until after midnight. Once, when me and Sharon were watching color TV in their living room, we heard Mrs. Bailey hollering a lot upstairs. I wanted to go see what was going on, but Sharon told me it was none of my business. I asked Mom and Dad why she was hollering, and they said she was just acting silly. Mrs. Bailey's husband was always on a business trip somewhere.

Sharon used to call me a scairdy cat, because I was scared to death of stupid things. The toy dog I had barked and hopped, and I cried like it was real. I got a toy devil for Christmas but I threw it in the heater because I had nightmares it was outside our bedroom window. Mom told me if I didn't go to sleep on Christmas Eve, Santa Claus would put red pepper in my eyes.

I only remember one Christmas on Blunt Street. Sharon got a big, fancy new doll that she [despised]. Sometimes she laid it on the floor and beat it in the back with a stick. Later she cut all of the hair off, and when Mom found out she gave her a bad whipping. Sharon hid Gitchy Lou under the mattress, because she was afraid Mom would take her and throw her away.

Everything scared me then. Road Drag Monsters [earth moving machines] and street sweepers were like Godzilla. But the thing that scared me the most was the Muskito Man.

The Muskito Man made a sound like a lawnmower. I would hear that lawnmower sound, and I would see the thick smoke cloud rising above the houses down the road.

Then I could see it was getting closer…

It appeared suddenly, with that fog of white smoke pouring out. I ran straight to the house. Sharon wouldn't unlock the screen door, and I was banging on it and begging her to please open it. When she unlocked it I ran in the house and watched the Muskito Man through the screen door.

Kids would be riding their bikes through it and playing in it like it was whipped cream. Even Sharon would run into it at full speed. It looked like she vanished into another dimension.

I was in kindergarten when we lived on Blunt Street. Kindergarten was weird. I get a creepy feeling when I think about it.

At recess, all the other kids ordered chocolate milk There was always one red carton in the crate every single day—my plain white milk. We hatched chickens in an incubator. We even hatched butterflies out of a chrysalis. We took trips to the planetarium and the zoo, and took care of hamsters. I stuck my finger too close once, and it bit me. I tried to pretend it didn't hurt, even though it left tooth marks on my finger.

We listened to records. Especially the one about the "dog that worried the cat that killed the rat that ate the malt that lay in the house that Jack built." And that stupid "Halloween is coming, ha ha ha" record. We listened to that dumb record a thousand times. Mom and Dad used to have a lot of [Beatles] records, but they threw them all away.

There were giant red, white and blue Leggo blocks that made too much noise when they fell. There was a boy name Rob that smelled like corn chips because he peed on himself and cried all the time. Another boy named José doo-dooed in his pants so much that we got used to the smell. He stunk every single day.

I remember always folding that thick construction paper, and cutting out hearts and snowflakes, and then opening it back up to see what it looked like. And it was always bad. I never got the shapes right. And I still don't know why Steve shook and fell that day when he and Otis crashed those metal firetrucks together. When I looked at them, he was shaking and falling to the ground like he had been hit with a baseball bat.

All I remember about my kindergarten teacher is her short red hair and freckled face. But I can remember two of those substitutes we had. One had a funny looking face and was always yelling at me about something. At naptime, when I was laying on that blue mat, she started yelling "put your head down!" I didn't even know she was talking to me until she had yelled it three times.

The other substitute reminded me of the ladies in the perfume section at the department store. When I asked her what she wanted me to do with something (I can't remember what it was), she stuck her face close to me and puckered her lips like she was going to kiss me. Then she said "Mmmm. My sweet little Sarah, you can put it in the corner, you can put it on the shelf, you can do anything you want to do with it." Her voice tingled my whole body.

Kindergarten was weird.

One of Sharon's friends tricked her into stealing 20 dollars out of Aunt Rose's purse one day. When Aunt Rose found out about it, she cried. Then she told Sharon she was going to have to whip her.

She didn't want to do it. She kept putting it off all day. We thought she had forgotten about it because so many hours had passed. But later that afternoon she called Sharon into the house and whipped her with a belt. She didn't even cry, but she looked really scared and confused. I remember thinking that Aunt Rose shouldn't have done it. Mom never found out that it happened.

Whenever Sharon gets angry, she gets very quiet. And sometimes, she'll wipe tears out of her eyes.

Once in the department store, she wanted Mom to buy her a pretty t-shirt, but she wouldn't. She started acting mean to Mom in the store, and Mom said, "you just wait 'til I get you outside."

Everything was fine while we were in the parking lot. But as soon as we got in the car, Mom put the top up, and she turned around towards the back seat, and started hitting her on the face and head as hard as she could.

Sharon covered her face, but Mom kept hitting her arms and her back. She called her a "pissy little brat."

While we were driving home, I looked at Sharon's face. She had a calm, serious look, like she wasn't thinking about anything, but tears were pouring down her cheeks. She wouldn't even sniff or wipe her face. I saw Mom glancing at her in the rearview mirror. Sharon was looking out the window as if nothing had happened. But her face was red and wet with tears.

That was the first time I saw her act that way.

omeone once wrote that religion is the "opiate of the masses."
Someone else was known to have not believed in a "God of theology who
rewards good and punishes evil."Both were geniuses in their own right,
perhaps blinded by the brilliance of their own intellect—drunk and dazed
with the wine of infinite self appreciation. And even though I sympathize
with skepticism, it bothers me that intelligence is more willing to accept the
idea of extraterrestrials, than even the possibility of a morally omnipotent
God-being.

With that over and done, I turn my thoughts back to my mother and father. But it should be made clear that their fanaticism and pseudo-righteousness bears little resemblance to the Truth. Their madness has not caused me to dismiss religion as invalid, nor God as aloof or nonexistent. But as time passes by, I have often found myself asking the bitter question, "Where was He, when my sister and me were suffering?"

There are things that they did to me in the name of religion—things that my mother did to me alone, in the deepest, darkest privacy of secret...even now, the pressure of anguish threatens to explode from this pen, to record some of the deepest pain she administered to my spirit. At this moment, I am actually afraid.

May God forgive me for remembering.

November 19ᵗʰ

What really happens when you die?

Last night, I think I was going to die. In my sleep I saw a city at night. And then, all of the lights started going out, like in a blackout. I knew it meant my brain was shutting down.

Then I saw my sister kneeling on one knee with her head down, like she was praying for me. I woke up in the middle of the night with a bad headache, and I had to pee. I went in the yellow bucket, and it was the strongest smelling [urine] I had ever smelled. It smelled like medicine.

Thanksgiving is this Thursday.

I already know they won't let me out. They'll probably eat Thanksgiving Dinner at somebody else's house. I should ask Mom to let me have the TV for just one day. Cartoons will be on in the morning, and then the parade will be on. It would give me something else to do.

She would have been sorry if I had died. Then she would want to take it all back, but it would be too late. She would be crying at my funeral, and wishing she could have me alive again.

I think that when we die, it's like falling asleep. After we fall asleep, our souls wake up when an angel calls us, and we fly to Heaven with the angel. We fly up past the moon and the stars, through the universe, and then into Heaven.

People who are evil won't go to Heaven when the angel calls. The angel will take them all the way down to Hell. Fire will be all around them, but they won't be burning yet. They'll be [tormented] by the heat from the flames, and they'll be very thirsty and afraid. Their tongues will be parched with thirst.

The angel will tell them why they're in Hell, even though they already know why. And then on Judgment Day, [he] will take them all the way to Heaven to be judged by God. God will show them every second of their life. The whole time, they'll be crying and complaining, but it won't do any good because they will see everything they did wrong. And then, God will tell the angel to see if their name appears in the Book of Life.

The angel will say "His name does not appear Lord."

Then God will say *"Depart from me, ye that worketh iniquity, into the everlasting fire prepared for the devil and his angels."* The angel will take that person back to Hell, and throw him into the Lake of Fire.

I think that a lot of preachers and church people aren't going to Heaven because they're just pretending.

On Valentines Day, Dad gave Mom a giant box of candy and a big [bouquet] of red roses. She started crying, and she kissed him. Sharon told me it almost made her sick to her stomach.

Mom was able to control her easily because of Dad. Dad always protected Mom, and did everything she said.

She once claimed that a bee had crawled down her dress. She was screaming and pulling at it, and Dad ran up to her and tore her dress off. I saw her in the front yard jiggling around in her bra and that torn dress. They didn't even find any bees, but she was kissing on him like he had just saved her life.

I've seen a picture of Mom holding Sharon when she was a baby. Mom was smiling and wearing a pretty pink housecoat.

Sharon was six when I was born. In all of her younger pictures, I can't tell if she's happy or sad. She never smiled in those pictures. There's no fakeness in her personality. Aunt Rose said she was a good child.

She could have done a lot of things. Maybe even played sports. Whenever she threw Dad's old football, the ball flew in a perfect spiral, like it floated out of her hands. At Aunt Rose's company field day, there was a football throw, and Sharon won a prize.

Cousin Craig was there too. He was calling me a string bean, and teasing me because I was too shy to throw. He kept sticking one of those old footballs in my face. It smelled like leather.

Sharon bumped into him so hard that he almost fell. He threw the ball at her face but she blocked it. Then he slapped her in the back of the head and she threw the ball at him and missed. She chased him halfway across that whole big meadow. He was laughing, but she wasn't.

Everybody started leaving the picnic because it was about to rain. When there was nobody around, I threw the football with no problem. I made it through the target a lot before Sharon came over to get me.

I just had to lay down for awhile. I got a flash of heat in my body, and I broke out into a sweat. My heart was beating real fast. I could feel the blood running through my body. I felt my life slipping away.

Death is cold and lonely. It's scarier than the worse pain I've ever felt. It feels like I'm going to slip out of life, and float into outer space. It's an echo of night and winter.

I want [Sharon] to come and take me out of this house. I'm going to tell her everything.

Maybe they aren't going to beat me up anymore. Maybe they got it all out of their system.

They don't pretend anymore. They act exactly how they feel. I think they see me as a pet. They feed me only because they have to. I only see hatred in my mother's eyes.

The next time she comes in, I'm going to ask her to let me go to church. I'm going to tell her how sorry I am that I was disobedient. I'm going to act right from now on. If they don't hurt me anymore, then I won't need to call my sister. At least things will be normal, and I won't be trapped like I'm inside a tomb.

I'm probably not going to die.

She gave me some left over meatloaf. It tasted spoiled so I couldn't eat it. Maybe if I put it on the roof, a bird will come down and take it away.

She ignored me when I tried to talk to her. She looked tired and depressed. I wanted to hug her, and tell her that everything was alright.

I asked her if I can go to church with them on Wednesday night. She just put the plate on the bed and walked out. She acted like I hadn't said a word.

I think she's unhappy because of me.

Why didn't she let me stay with Aunt Rose? Why did she bring me here? They don't even need me.

I can hear her getting ready to take a bath. She always stays in there forever. If they go to a restaurant tonight, she'll wear her makeup.

She used to have a lot of different kinds of lipstick. There were a bunch of perfume bottles on her dresser, and a big box of jewelry. The box was made of wood, and it was lined with burgundy [velvet] cloth. She kept her earrings and rings in it. It was full of gold necklaces and bracelets.

Aunt Rose's jewelry box was different. It was full of big dress pins, and there were so many pearl necklaces that they used to stay tangled up in knots. They looked like marbles. She had a beautiful [porcelain] swan close to the mirror. She has every color of roses growing beside her house. The one on her dresser is coated in pure gold. It's in a crystal vase. Sharon wouldn't let me touch it. She said it was too perfect.

Mom is not a good housewife. She doesn't care about decorating. This place reminds me of a haunted house. When you drive up to it at night, it looks too big and scary to go in. It looked condemned when we first got here.

When you first walk in, there's a scary hallway that leads to a door. After you go through the door, there is a flight of stairs. The stairs lead to another flight, then up to this second floor hallway.

My room is the smallest bedroom. Its in the middle of the hall, down from Mom and Dad's room.

Every time Mom goes somewhere in the house, I hear her walking past my door. I wonder a lot if she's going to stop. Sometimes I get scared when she walks by. Other times, I feel hope.

She is still in the bathroom. I can hear the water running. That bathroom is so old that it doesn't even have a shower. It has an old fashioned bathtub.

If I get too hungry, I might have to eat this meatloaf. If I had ketchup it would be better.

Mom didn't inherit Grandma's cooking ability.

I had expected them to argue before they left. But they seemed very quiet. It was almost like they were afraid I would hear what they were saying. They've been gone for a long time. It's very dark outside.

The next time Mom comes in, I'll ask her to let me have the TV back.

November 20ᵗʰ

Once, I asked my mother why did we become poor. She said that God called them to be poor. She said that some people are meant for suffering.

I think that maybe I'm meant for suffering.

I know I can't ask them for another thing, and I know I won't ever escape from this house. My head hurts so bad that I can hardly think. It feels like I need to go to sleep.

She stood by the door and watched it happen. It was almost 12:30 last night. I heard them arguing when they got home. I knocked on the door when they walked by and asked them could I please have the TV back.

I think that was the worst whipping I ever got. As soon as he took off his belt I started crying. I begged him to please don't whip me. I couldn't believe they were going to whip me again.

It felt like my skin was being cut.

I went straight to bed when it was over. I didn't want to look at it, but I could feel the welts all over my body.

I thought a lot about Mom while Dad was hitting me. I know she caused it, but I just wanted her to help me. She just stood there and watched it happen. I haven't done anything wrong, have I? What did I do?

There are dark bruises all over my body, and a lot of places where the belt cut into my skin.

Tomorrow, I'm going to remember my big sister. I'm going to write as much as I know, and everything I remember about all the pain she suffered in this family.

This is happening to me because Sharon isn't here.

Because she couldn't take it anymore.

The House on Sycamore Avenue

To me belongeth vengeance, and recompense; for the day of their calamity is at hand...

Deuteronomy 32: 35

he darkness that had loomed for years descended, with power and purpose of intent. After I turned 16, my mother began to take every opportunity to make me ashamed of my body. Through no fault of my own, I suppose that my figure was more noticeable than it needed to be, and the self-consciousness it warranted was inherent. A girl at that age is poised on a razor's edge between confidence and insecurity, and each look, each glance, each whispered word has the potential power of gale force winds, to send her careening helplessly in either direction.

My mother's lustful obsession with my body seemed to grow in proportion with it. She tapped into fear's energy, drew strength from the power of pain, infusing me with the dread she needed to dominate my spirit. I lived in terror of the brutal punishments, and the twisted things she had begun to inflict upon every part of my being.

May God have mercy on me, and upon all of those who have endured, and can conceive of the hurt from whence I speak.

November 21ˢᵗ

Sharon was sixteen years old when we moved from the tiny house on Blunt Street. I remember the day we moved because we were all so happy. She was a sophomore in high school, and she was old enough to get her driver's license.

I felt lucky that day. Dad was a good schoolteacher that everybody liked, and Mom was pretty and everybody loved her. And we were moving into a big, beautiful house. I was glad we were leaving that old neighborhood. I don't think I ever really liked it there. That house makes me think about snakes, wasps, and dead cats.

She could have sat with Mom in her car. Or she could have sat with Dad up front in that old station wagon.

I never felt luckier, than when she looked back at me and said, "I'm going to sit with Sarah." She climbed over the seat like a happy little girl, even though she was already starting to look like a grown woman. Her hair was long, golden yellow, and she was wearing a white button down shirt and faded blue jeans. Her eyes were blue.

I was lucky, because that was the day I found out she really liked me, and she wasn't faking. We were both in the back of the station wagon, looking out the back window.

I remember watching the small old houses go by. The car went down a steep hill while we drove around the block, past the woods. We passed over the creek that ran deep into those woods where we used to play. The last thing we passed was the little store where we would walk to buy ice cream and candy.

The new place we were going seemed farther away than it really was. I can see all the pretty trees in my mind. It seemed like we were going to a better place.

I was lucky, because she hugged me and touched my hair with her lips. But I was afraid to look at her. I never wanted her to [tease] me or start calling me names. But she only said "So sweet and quiet." I turned and looked at her, and she crossed her eyes and leaned her forehead against mine. Then she whispered in my ear.

I looked at her again, but she wasn't smiling or acting silly. She wanted me to know that she really loved me. I could see it on her face. I could feel it.

I felt lucky that day, when we moved from the house on Blunt Street.

Sycamore Avenue was very pretty. There were a lot of flowers and trees. We had already seen it a lot, but we never thought we would be living there. That day, it looked even better.

The neighborhood was much nicer. The houses were bigger, and they didn't look old like the one I was born in. There was a small library across the street from our new house. It was a little brick building with a big window in the front. I can't remember how many days I spent there. It had a record with music from the Wizard of Oz. The librarian let me listen to it all the time.

It was a big, white house with no upstairs. The front yard was small, but there was a huge backyard with a big pecan tree, and a grapevine. Mom called them "country grapes." The skin was so thick that you could only eat the inside. There was a small tree too, that made some kind of yellow fruit that tasted like plums. The front porch had a screen on part of it, where we could sit in chairs and watch cars go by.

If I told Sharon the things Mom has done, I think I know what would happen.

Moving day was the first time we were inside the house together. I had been there with Dad once already, and I had my room all picked out, until Sharon saw it.

"Oh no you don't", she said.

I should have known better. She said she was the oldest, so she was taking the big bedroom. For some reason, I thought she would want the smaller one. It seemed more private. Dad said "I told you she wouldn't let you have it."

Dad liked TV's so much that we had five of them. Sharon and me both had one in our room. Dad had one in his bedroom. And there were two TV's in the living room. One of them was a big floor model color TV, but it broke down, and Dad never got it fixed. The day we left Williamston, that TV was on the side of the road in a pile of junk.

On our first night in the new house, we drove to a restaurant, and we brought the food back home. Sharon had fried shrimp, and I had chicken because I hate shrimp. We ate together in her room, while Mom and Dad ate in the kitchen.

We had shared a room every day since I was little. That was the first night we had ever slept in our own room.

The world is raining again. The trees are starting to die for the winter.

Our early days on Sycamore Avenue were good. Even the cold winter skies were blue. Things had started to change a little, but there was always hope.

There was still hope, even after Dad first walked into the house that night, singing a strange song in tongues. We found out he had visited the Holiness Church for the first time. Mom and Dad had never gone to church before that night. I can remember him hugging us a lot for days. Me and Sharon would laugh at him sometimes.

He took Mom to church soon after.

They started making me and Sharon go to church with them all the time after that. They made us go to the altar the first day we got there. I obeyed the preacher but I don't know if I'm really saved because I never spoke in tongues.

Sharon was baptized that Sunday afternoon. Mom told her that she was going to [tarry] for the [Baptism of the Holy Spirit] the next Sunday night.

At that Sunday night alter call, some of the other people started going back to their seats after a while. I was going to ask Sharon if we could go back, but she was crying. I glanced at Mom, and she said I could go sit down. When I got back to my seat, I looked at Mom and Sharon.

I saw Sharon with her hands in the air, and her eyes were closed. She was [praising God] over and over. A lot of women were standing around her praying. Mom was just staring at her. It was like she was [studying her] to see if she was faking. She had a frown on her face.

Another woman touched Mom, and her frown went away. Mom was shaking her head like she thought Sharon was hopeless. After a while, Sharon started to jump a little, and I saw her hands trembling. The ladies were all yelling so loud that I didn't hear her speak in tongues, but later she told me she did.

Mom whispered something in Sharon's ear, and helped her back to her seat. Sharon's face was very sad, like she was crying from misery instead of joy.

Sharon got filled with the Holy [Spirit] that night. It should have helped her to get along with Mom. It should have helped her to be happy.

Things started to get really bad after that. Mom and her were arguing all the time. We got punished for every little thing, and her punishments began to get worse and worse. They both hurt her a lot, but Mom hurt her more often.

When Mom whipped her or spanked her, she was able to keep from crying sometimes. She would just breathe hard, and grunt like an animal. I could hear her straining and letting herself get angry, so she wouldn't cry.

The first thing that happened on Sycamore Avenue was about her license. I couldn't wait until she got them, because she would take me everywhere she went. Sharon had already been upset about it, because they said she could get them on her birthday, but they had lied.

I was in the backyard that day, in the shade of the pecan tree. I wish I was there now in the green, under the blue sky. I loved to throw my softball up into that tree and watch it hit branches on the way down. It made it more fun to try and catch.

All of a sudden, I heard them arguing really loud. It kind of scared me because they were both very angry. I had never heard them argue like that before. I could see through the screen, and I saw Sharon yelling at Mom as if she was her age.

I sneaked around to the front of the house. The whole time, I was hoping they would stop. I wanted things to be different.

When I went in the living room, the house didn't feel right inside. It was quiet and I could hear something happening. I heard Mom hitting her. It was like little slapping noises. I went into the big den, and I saw it.

Mom had Sharon pressed up against the refrigerator, holding her around the throat and pulling her hair. Every now and then, she would slap her a couple of times and look at her, and say things to her so low that I couldn't hear. Sharon had her eyes closed with a hurt, angry look on her face. Mom just stayed pressed up against her. I think she slapped her at least ten times before she let her go. Then she said quietly "and just wait 'til your father gets home."

I hid while Mom walked to her bedroom. When I went in the kitchen, I saw Sharon at the sink looking out the window. She was hitting her fist on her thigh and crying. Her face was red from where Mom had been slapping her. When she looked at me I started to walk away, but she said "Where are you going?"

I don't know why she was trying to pretend it didn't happen.

I asked her what was the matter, and she just put her hands on her hips and took a deep breath.

"Is Mom going to let you get your license?"

"I don't know," [she said.] "It doesn't matter. Do you want to go get ice cream?"

"Where?"

"At the old store. It's not that far."

When she went to ask Mom could we get ice cream, I heard Mom yell something at her. I wish I could remember. I can see it in my mind, and I can hear her voice, but I can't make out what she was saying. Sharon came back into the kitchen and sat down at the table.

"Do you want to go to the library?" [I asked.]

"Let's go out back."

Before too long, it looked like she was having fun. I'll bet she was just covering up. But we both felt a little better.

Suddenly, I saw Mom at the back door. It made me overthrow the ball because I was nervous. Sharon walked onto the porch to get it, and her smile disappeared, and she was fiddling with her hair.

In that split second, she looked like a grown woman, trapped playing catch with a little girl to try to be happy.

I watched close to see if they were going to start arguing some more. Sharon came back in the yard, and we were playing catch with the rubber softball again.

A few minutes later, Mom came out. The wind was blowing her long, pretty blue dress while she went to her white [convertible]. That car was so much better than the one we have now.

Sometimes, Mom seemed like a stranger.

As soon as she drove away, Sharon took the softball and threw it at the kitchen window. It hit the wood and cracked one of the window panes.

My sister was a quiet girl, who liked to read and do her schoolwork. It seemed that when she turned sixteen, her [bosoms] started to get very large. Once, I told her "those things are too big, Sharon. They're bigger than Mom's." She just laughed and said "How would you know? Have you been looking, pervert?" Then she hollered like Bugs Bunny does when he gets caught in the shower.

I think she might have been the smartest one in our family. She got all A's. She wasn't in any [honors] clubs or smart classes, but she was still a good student.

"Let's go for a walk," she said.

We left the yard for a while, and took a stroll. There was a long, quiet path a few blocks away. There were plenty of tall shade trees, and it seemed very private. We were lucky because we seemed to be the only ones who ever went. When grown people rode by on bikes, Sharon said they didn't know how stupid they looked. There was a bench, and sometimes we sat there together for a long time. We didn't care if Mom came back and saw that we weren't in the yard.

Mom said it wasn't God's will for her to get a license yet. She had to wait until she was 21. She said they were going to keep her here "for as long as it took," whatever that meant. Even while she told me about it, she started crying.

I think I was glad she didn't have a license. I know she would have been gone a lot if they let her drive. They never let her go anywhere. She wasn't even allowed to go to her friend's houses anymore. I don't know if she really had any friends.

Mom and Dad had her trapped in a cage.

When Dad called her to their bedroom that afternoon, I knew she was in trouble. I could feel it, and my nerves were on edge. But she didn't seem worried. She just wondered what in the world they could possibly want.

It was the first time I ever heard it happen.

It scared me every time, but the first time was the worse. I can remember her starting to talk loud in their bedroom about how sorry she was. I don't know if it was happening because of the window, or the way she had back-talked Mom.

I heard Sharon say, "What are you doing? Mom please don't let this happen!"

The fear in her voice was very strong. It felt like it was happening to me. I heard Mom tell her to shut her rebellious mouth and do as she asked. She was crying softly for a few minutes, and then it started.

There was a lot of banging around in the room, and she started to scream like she was being burned alive. I have no idea how long they hurt her, but she screamed forever. It would stop for a while, and then it would start again.

I knew exactly how she felt. I know how it feels when they burn your skin, and you can't breathe anymore because of the pain.

Sharon was the only one who came out of the bedroom. She was in her underwear, and she was crying. She was holding her clothes. I wanted her to talk to me, so I didn't look away. A few marks were on her thighs and arms, but when she walked to her room, I saw what they had done to her.

Her back was covered with burns, from her neck down to the back of her legs. Her bra was unfastened. Some of the skin had spots of blood, and there were dark bruises all over. The back of her underwear had [streaks] of dried blood. It seemed like all of her skin was damaged.

She just ignored me, and went into her room. I heard her crying as if the pain had started again.

She didn't come to eat supper. She didn't come out of her room anymore the whole night. When Mom asked me did we go anywhere that day, I froze from the inside out. I told them we walked to the bench down the bike path, but they didn't say anything. It felt like someone had put a gun to my face, and then took it away.

I think they had used [a curling iron] on her back. But I don't know.

November 22nd [Thanksgiving Day]

I know she is thinking about me. She knows that my holiday is unhappy.

Maybe she's writing me a long letter right now. I don't know if she's written me since school started, because Mom told me to never touch the mail. But whenever I got a chance to sneak and look inside, there were no letters for me.

I hope she will have a long, happy life. I hope that she won't cry when I'm gone.

My dreams are all so scary now. Last night I dreamed that I made it to the highway leading to Williamston, but the road was flooded as far as I could see, like an ocean. Mom and Dad were gone when I woke up this morning. I'll probably get to sleep even before they get home tonight.

I used to tease kids who acted like nobody cared about them. But I swear I'll never do it again. Everyone has at least one person who really cares about them. But the one who cares about me isn't here. I don't have anybody left.

"Honor thy father and thy mother, that thy days may be long upon the land which the Lord thy God giveth thee."

I know I'm not supposed to hate [Mom]. Maybe that's why I'm suffering, because I've been hating her in my heart. If I try to honor her, then my punishment will stop.

They think I'm going to cry because I don't have any food. She didn't even give me anything to drink. But the rainwater is cold, and I'm not thirsty anyway.

It feels like pure winter today. I could see my breath when I opened the window.

I might not get a chance to see Sharon again. I feel so cold, but I don't want to die. I'm so afraid that I'm going to die.

Death is like an icy river, moving through the warm land of the living. It flows from a mountain of darkness, into the valley of light.

I think that a person can get used to being afraid. But I still don't look in the mirror at night anymore. I keep a blanket over it at night, because it seems like a witch's shadow lives in there. I've seen it in my sleep, but it didn't feel like a dream.

Why does evil come into the world? How does it happen?

Evil is like a parasite. It lives inside people, and feeds on them. Their soul is infected by it when they are born.

I don't have a good feeling about things.

But I don't want to die.

I listen when people talk about Heaven, and I can hear that they don't understand it. They act like it's a golden ghost city in the clouds, with angels and phantoms floating around.

But Heaven is a real place. A place that can be seen and touched. But only spirits and souls can ever see it. When we die, Heaven will be more real to us than this world ever was. It will be like waking up into [reality], instead of dying out of it.

I want to live there when I die. Tonight I'm going to pray for my soul, to make sure He will take me.

When I look out into the rain, I feel very strange. I feel like I'm in mourning for the death of a loved one.

There's no thunder in a November rain. It's always very quiet... and peaceful.

*I*n all of my life, through the endless searching for purpose, reason and justification, I have found only this—that where the will of man ends, God's Will begins, and you cannot change what is meant to be. But still, I wish I could understand why fate deemed it necessary to take her. Maybe she would have accomplished something in the world, something significant, that simply was not supposed to happen. It is a question that truly, I can never know the answer to.

Perhaps there is only Fate, Destiny, and the Will of God.

November 23rd

Last night, I dreamed that Sharon was standing outside of Aunt Rose's church in the middle of a big crowd. Everybody was happy except her. But her hair was golden, and she was wearing the most beautiful long black leather coat I've ever seen. She walked through the crowd and got into a black limousine and rode away. It looked like she had become rich, but she seemed very sad.

After her first punishment in the new house, we both began to wish we lived with Aunt Rose. I knocked on her bedroom door the next day.

"Is that you Sarah?"

She had started to keep her door closed all the time. She didn't watch TV much anymore. She began to read more books, and her radio was always on the classical music station.

Sharon told me they did it because she had disrespected Mom. They said she was full of the Devil, and that they were going to burn it out of her if it took them two years to do it.

I don't think Mom was ever going to let us go back to Aunt Rose's house. She didn't say it but I know that's what she was planning. We were lucky that school was out, because she couldn't use it as an excuse to keep us from going over there.

Sharon wished they would just leave her alone to read and watch TV, and not make her work all the time, and punish her for every little thing.

She never had any friends over to Aunt Rose's. It was almost like she didn't really know anybody. She was always with Aunt Rose or reading magazines. She was different over there. More relaxed.

We were supposed to be home by ten o'clock whenever we went to her house. But once when we went shopping out of town, we didn't get home until after eleven o'clock. Mom was so mad that she made us stay in for a whole week. She didn't even let us go over there the next Friday.

Aunt Rose showed up at our house that Friday night. She found out that we were on punishment. But when she found out why, she asked us could we let her talk to Mom alone for a minute. I heard her yelling at Mom like she was her mother instead of her sister. After a few minutes Dad even went into the kitchen. I heard him say "Rosa Lee I think you've said enough." Aunt Rose was so mad she couldn't hardly talk to us when she left.

She came to get us every Friday after that. But Mom started letting us walk again after a while. It was probably because she didn't want to see Aunt Rose. Every Friday afternoon, Mom was as angry as a red wasp.

Only Dad calls her Rosa Lee. I tried to call her Aunt Rose before, but she wouldn't let me. She would probably do great on a farm. She's a strong woman. She has a curved shape and big giant [bosoms]. Sharon's body is a smaller version.

I think Mom was jealous of Sharon. She was always accusing her of "walking around and sticking her big chest out." After a while, Sharon stopped tucking her shirts in. She acted like she was embarrassed.

They argued so much about what she wore. But Sharon was learning not to get too sassy.

Mom had worn pants for years. But one day, she packed all of her pants and button down collar shirts into garbage bags, and threw them away. She sold all of her jewelry, except for her wedding ring.

Sharon had always worn blue jeans. She had over 20 pairs of jeans and pants and shorts. But when she found out what Mom had done to her own clothes, I'm sure she knew what was coming. It probably appeared in her brain like a creature, and spread fear to her body.

They went into Sharon's room one night, and took all of her jeans and shorts away. They threw all of them into the middle of the floor, and made her put them in black trash bags. When she finished, she went into the bathroom. I expected to hear her crying, but she didn't make a sound. She stayed in there until Mom banged on the door and asked what she was doing. She just came out and went back to her room, and slammed the door so hard I thought she was going to get punished.

The more I remember her, the more I understand.

She got more and more depressed that summer. She didn't have anybody else but Aunt Rose, and we only saw her once a week. It was our first summer on Sycamore Avenue.

Mom says that Aunt Rose looks like a Jezebel.

At the end of that summer, we found out that Dad was going to quit teaching [after 13 years]. Everybody was shocked, because he was such a good teacher. Mom had already quit her job at the elementary school. She said she dreamed they would get killed in a car accident if he didn't stop teaching.

So he quit teaching the 10th grade, and got a job driving a bread truck. I liked it because we got so many free snacks. We always had every kind of snack and cake I can imagine. Mom used to say that her hips were going to suffer, but she didn't gain a single pound. She hardly ate any of it.

Dad threw away his fishing equipment. He stopped going hunting too. He went up into the attic and brought down his rifle, and then he broke it. I can remember the wood splitting while he was doing it.

He sold the convertible and the motorcycle. He said they were both sinful because they looked too worldly.

We began to visit a lot of people's houses that summer. People all over Williamston that I had never met. Sharon wanted to stay home sometimes, but they always made her come with us. Thank goodness, because I hated going to those houses. Sometimes they would have church services.

We started visiting Rocky Mount two years before we moved here. We would even spend the night with people. Sometimes I heard loud praying until late at night. I would wake up in the middle of the night and wonder where in the world I was. We have slept on a lot of uncomfortable couches and floors.

I noticed that everybody we visited were always [in poverty]. All of Mom and Dad's old friends seemed rich. But I didn't like visiting their new friends. They all had fireplaces or wood heaters, and the houses always smelled like smoke and kerosene. Dad always seemed to be outside chopping wood with them if it was daylight, and Mom was always inside cooking or babysitting. Sometimes they had children our age. It was miserable getting to know them, because I just wanted to go home.

But the worst place I remember was a small farm. They had a tiny little house, and it smelled like a hog everywhere on that whole property. They lived so far in the country it was like another planet, especially at night. A lonely older couple lived there. They acted so glad we came to visit. I could tell they needed some company. They lived in the middle of nowhere.

There was a mushroom growing in the corner on their back porch. There was a big hole in the living room wall. I could see the wood underneath the plaster. Their couch had holes in it with the foam showing. The bathroom wasn't in the house. Sharon said she would piss her pants before she would ever go in that outhouse. We ate pigs tails for supper there once, and they made every one of us sick.

Dad liked to drive out with Mr. Dallas to his cornfield. Sharon and me would look at the chickens. There were all colors of chickens living together. We watched his wife feed the pigs, and all I could think about was what if I fell in the pig pen. We made homemade ice cream once, and it was terrible. Mr. Dallas ate four bowls.

I'm glad we never spent the night on that farm.

November 24th

We were glad to finally start school that year. Sharon was in the tenth grade. It was our first school year in the new house. But hope was vanishing away.

Early one morning, Mom woke me up, and told me that Dad was in an accident, and was at the hospital. She was acting nice, like she wanted to make sure I wasn't afraid.

When we got to the hospital, Dad was sitting on the edge of the hospital bed with bloody stitches in his forehead. There was a creepy mood in there. It was like we were in a gray fog.

We found out his delivery truck had been hit by an 18-wheeler truck. It had run a red light and slammed right into him. He said he had never worn his seatbelt before that morning.

His other accident was even stranger. He was making a delivery near Virginia when it happened. He was driving full speed down the highway, and the [whole rear axle] came off his truck while he was driving. But he didn't even get hurt. After the second accident, Dad got fired.

I still remember his work picture. He was wearing a blue shirt and holding a loaf of bread. He looked happy, even though it was a terrible picture, and it made that little round scar on his forehead look even worse. He got that scar because he fell into a wood stove when he was a little boy, and it burned the skin off.

He went to work in a convenience store after he got fired. Sometimes he worked all night long. It's a miracle he never got robbed, because that store was in a bad neighborhood. One day he sat down at the kitchen table and looked at his paycheck, and he was shaking his head.

After that, he got a job at a fish market. It was cold outside everyday when he came home. He always stank up the whole house with that smell. He got fired from that job too.

He was unemployed for a long time. That was the first time we got our lights cut off. But Mom acted like she didn't even care. We were visiting so many people's houses that it didn't seem to matter.

Mom told us she would skin us alive if we told Aunt Rose about the lights. It scared us to death every time she brought us home, until the lights finally came back on. She even said "That stingy Linda won't even burn the porch lights for you." I think that maybe Sharon would have told her about it, if I hadn't begged her not to.

We had to burn candles at night if we wanted to see. Mom and Dad kept the kerosene lamp in their room. There was no heat, and it was winter. Our neighborhood was [the suburbs], and I know everybody else had money, except us.

One of those cold nights, Sharon asked me to sleep in her bed. Mom got angry when she found out, and she wouldn't let me sleep with Sharon any more. She acted like we had done something wrong.

In the spring, Dad went to work at a grocery store. He came home sometimes wearing a red apron. He was wearing that apron once when Mom made him whip me. Whenever I got a whipping, Sharon always came to my room and hugged me.

I'm used to not eating much food now. Sometimes she doesn't bring me anything, but I don't care anymore. My stomach growls all the time, and I'm not even hungry.

My [journal] is hidden very well. Nobody will ever find it.

13

There were times when the worst of it happened, that I clearly detected the faintest scent of alcohol. Yes, my mother did consume red wine in private. Even through the strict religious ritual and dedication, she maintained and nurtured this vice, sometimes to completion. But whether or not she felt guilty or begged for absolution, this I will never know.

When I was 17, she would pull me over her lap in the name of discipline, and spank my buttocks like I was a child, until I was crying and begging for her to stop. Sometimes my skin was badly bruised, many times with my father having watched it happen. When she was particularly angry, she would hold my arms up behind my back, while my father gave me the severest paddling imaginable. I found these impossible to endure, and the pain made it difficult for me to walk for days afterwards. I cannot bear the thought that Sarah may have sometimes heard my pathetic screaming and pleading for mercy.

A sexual undercurrent flowed beneath most of the scores of punishments she administered to me. But the depth of her perversions might go beyond what many are prepared to believe or understand. The misery I felt after each incident was unfathomable. Worse than the pain of the most brutal beatings.

But my mother was not insane. She was perhaps the most rational and socially well adjusted person I ever knew.

November 25th

Sharon was 17 in our last school year together. I think maybe it was the worst year of her life.

One day, her school called Mom at the house, and told her she had skipped class and was caught smoking [marijuana] with a bunch of other girls. I remember coming home from school that day, and she was sitting on my bed in her long skirt. She was acting brave, but I knew she was scared because she was in my room instead of hers.

When Dad got home, they sat her down in the living room, and they all talked for a long time. Sharon was telling them she swore to God she wasn't smoking, but they didn't believe her. I don't know if she was lying or not.

I had already heard a lot of the whippings and spankings she got. Whenever she got hit with the paddle, she would be screaming so loud and deep I had to cover my ears.

Dad came and told me to go in the living room. I thought they were going to ask me a question. Mom told me to sit down. A new pack of cigarettes was on the table.

"I want you to see this," [Mom said,] so you'll know what will happen to you if you get caught smoking."

She made Sharon take off her shirt and her long skirt. She was standing embarrassed, right in front of all three of us. Mom tied her legs together with a cloth, and Dad told her to get on the floor on her hands and knees. Then he held her head by the ears like she was a dog. Mom held the belt in her hand like a cowboy holds a whip.

She raised it up and hit Sharon across her back as hard as she could. She kept hitting her across her whole body. Sharon was shaking and breathing fast on her knees. She was trying not to make any noise because I was in there.

But after a while it was too much for her, because her back was so red and bruised. She screamed a loud scream of pure pain, but it sounded like she was too angry to be sorry. I know it hurt because I saw spit fall out of her mouth. When I think about it, I can imagine the purplish color I see when they do it to me.

Mom beat her until she broke down and started begging Jesus to help her. But that just made Mom angrier. She had an strange look in her eyes. Like quiet anger. It took a long time, but Sharon finally started crying like she was sorry. Mom was too angry. Dad had to call her name loud to make her stop.

Then Dad opened the cigarettes, and lit one of them.

They made her lay flat on her stomach. Dad sat on her back, and Mom sat on her legs. Then she put the hot cigarette on Sharon's back. She screamed again. A very sad and pitiful scream, like she had given up hope.

After they burned her, they made her get to her knees and ask God to forgive her sins. They made me do it too. And Mom stood in front of us and prayed for us. She laid her hands on our foreheads. But all I could think about was the blood on Sharon's skin. When it was over, they made her stand up and read Bible verses about children being [beaten] with a rod as punishment.

That night, I had a nightmare that little pieces of wood were stuck in Sharon's back.

They didn't let her go to Aunt Rose's house for weeks. I had to walk over there by myself.

When I told her that Sharon was on punishment, it felt like my body turned to ice. There was no way I was going to tell her what happened in that living room. I was glad she didn't ask me. We went shopping a lot those weeks when Sharon wasn't there. She brought me a lot of pretty dresses then.

Being at Aunt Rose's house without Sharon was different. It was empty.

Mom and Dad were becoming like Jesus People. They prayed and read the Bible all the time. They went to church four times a week. Mom's hair started growing longer and darker.

They sometimes had church services in the house. We had to sit and sing and clap, then stand up and [give testimony]. They would make Sharon stand up and read long Bible verses. I think I know "Lazarus and the Rich Man" and "The Good Samaritan" and "The Prodigal Son" by heart now.

When Mom was a teacher, she dressed nice every day. She wore makeup and pretty earrings, and her makeup made her look more beautiful than everybody. Aunt Rose said Dad was such a good teacher that he should have been a principal.

But things had changed. We hardly ever had any money. They started to make me and Sharon wear long dresses and skirts every day, and they didn't let her get involved in any school activities. They wouldn't even let her join the [National Honor Society], and the only time we got to play outside was once a week.

Sometimes, Mom's friends would bring their little children over, and Sharon had to babysit them. She had to clean their stinky cloth diapers, and give them a bath and cook and feed all of us. She wore an apron, and she stood with her hands on her hips like Aunt Rose. I liked those times because it felt like she was my mother, and she never yelled at me. But she yelled at those other kids a whole lot. Mom and Dad would stay away until 2:00 in the morning on Friday nights.

Those little kids were a ~~nusince~~ nuisance. We couldn't enjoy the TV or do our homework in peace and quiet when they were there. Sometimes, Sharon got angry with them and made them all sit in the living room and watch TV. When they left, it felt like a tornado had passed.

Sharon didn't seem quite as afraid as she used to.

At school, she got a lot of detentions, and she was having a lot of fights. It seemed like she got in a fight at least once a week. She said it was because girls were always teasing her about her clothes. A group of black girls jumped her once, and one of them had to go to the hospital for a broken nose. I remember that there was blood on Sharon's shirt that day.

She almost got [expelled] for pushing one of her teachers. The teacher fell back against the desk but she didn't get hurt. They said the only reason she didn't get expelled is because she was a straight A student.

Whenever Dad wasn't around, it was almost for certain she and Mom were going to start arguing. They never had anything nice to say. They hated each other like a cat and a dog. The only way Mom could make her be quiet was to grab her and slam her against the wall and threaten to make Dad "beat the blood out of her."

I was in my room one night, hanging up a poster I ordered from school. They were fussing again, like always.

All of a sudden they got real quiet. Then I heard a plate fall on the floor and break. I looked in the kitchen from my bedroom, and Mom had her bent forward on the table with her arm pulled up behind her back. Sharon had a smarty pants look on her face on purpose, but Mom was mad. She was yelling to the top of her lungs "You will shut your mouth!"

Sharon acted like it wasn't even hurting her arm. I think she was glad she made Mom that angry. It's a good thing they didn't see me because Sharon doesn't know what I saw next.

Mom pulled her up by the hair. Then she grabbed Sharon's [breast] and twisted it as hard as she could. Sharon's face got serious, and she looked like she was going to push Mom away, until she screamed "Do you want me to tell your Father!" She screamed it over and over again but Sharon wouldn't answer.

Then Mom started hitting her on the shoulders and back, and pushing her like she was trying to start a fight. But Sharon just walked out of the kitchen to her room. Mom was behind her, pushing her in the back with all her might. Sharon slammed her bedroom door, and Mom couldn't make her unlock it.

The Autumn leaves are falling to the ground. The trees have gone to sleep for another winter.

Each time it happened, she did her best to inject the pretense with truth, that what was occurring was not the product of her sin, but rather the recompense that was due. But she kept it under the umbrella of discipline, whether for something I did, or was perhaps going to do. Private punishments. Private perversions that would give any psychiatrist enough fuel to burn curiosity for many years.

Mercifully, my sister was spared the indignity of knowing that my mother often stripped me of every stitch of fabric, and tied my arms and legs so completely that escape would have been impossible. Then she would stuff my mouth with a handkerchief and gag me with another one, to contain my screaming.

She would go into the back of her wardrobe and retrieve a black, flexible caning rod. Not a switch removed from some unfortunate birch tree, but a sturdy synthetic, perhaps fiberglass, that always welted and cut my skin to pieces with hardly any effort.

She often laid the cane on the bed, then disrobed before my eyes. Through blurred vision, I watched her with my mouth and hands bound, feeling the tears pour down my face as she removed her long dress, then removed her slip and her bra. During every caning, she left her underwear on, though she would often slide them very low on her hips. The nearly epic satisfaction in her eyes was terrifying.

She would hit me hard across the breasts or the buttocks, which made me draw in a breath through my nose, and another blow sent fire into my lungs and out through my muffled voice. I would scream and shake for dear life as she striped me bloody on my breasts, or from my hips to the bottom of my thighs.

This darkness began when I was seventeen, continuing for many months until it became something I expected. Whenever my father was away I laid in bed at night, trembling at the sound of her footsteps, shaking at the thought that she may have had another dream that told her I was developing a lustful, rebellious heart.

And there are many other things that I endured from my mother that are simply too horrible to mention. Things I cannot indulge, involving my body, and my chastity. I can only say that she took the most sacred part of me, perhaps that part that makes a woman the most special, the most worthy of love and respect. She filled my body with winter, ripping into me, and tearing my soul into bloody shreds. Terror's truth screamed from the pit of my stomach, through my lungs and my throat, spilling into my bleak and hopeless future. There were times when I shrieked a death scream into the walls of that accursed bedroom. Yes, I understand every particle of that desire to lose one's self—to disconnect one's being from the consciousness of a hellish reality.

But for the accursed, for every living thing there is shared a common gift. A focal point of strength in the midst of prolonged suffering. It is the knowledge that time will pass, and that all things must pass away. And every abuser, every condemned soul by whom the offence cometh fails to remember the one fact about the pain they cause:

Eventually, the suffering makes the victim stronger.

November 26th

I don't hate them anymore. I want to tell them I still love them.

I wish I could go back in time and help them not make the mistakes they made. Maybe even warn them not to come here. I feel like we're under a curse. The world itself might be under a curse.

Last night I dreamed that a meteor crashed into the Moon. Lava covered the whole thing, then it exploded into a billion fiery red pieces. If I could draw, I would paint the scene just like I saw it in my dreams.

It was a [cataclysm].

They really started to like Rocky Mount. People were always inviting them to church, their houses and to dinner. After a while, they were driving up here almost every night. Sharon was complaining about having time to do her homework. They came up here so much that they started leaving me and her home, except on Sundays.

Just after this Easter, they told us we were going to move to Rocky Mount at the end of the school year. We were going to have to change schools and leave all our friends. And we would never be able to walk to Aunt Rose's house again.

I can remember her and Sharon talking about it.

"Why can't we stay here with you, Aunt Janine?"

"Sharon, you already know what she's going to say."

"Will you just please ask her anyway?"

"Okay, but you know how Linda is. She'll never let you stay."

She did ask, and Mom said no. I'm sure Aunt Rose didn't even yell at her. And I know the look on Mom's face was pure pleasure.

We didn't want to have to move to this place. We had already been coming up here for a year, and it was always dreary. It looked like Fall every day when we came here. The trees were scraggly. Dead leaves were in the yards. The houses were small and raggedy. The [inner] city buildings were dingy and old looking. The office buildings were tall and scary. The whole city had a spirit of violence and misery.

Sharon hated having to spend her senior year in a new school. She had grown up with everybody since kindergarten. We were comfortable in our small town. When I think of it, it reminds me of blue skies, fluffy white clouds and summer breezes.

My life is like the sky above. Only every now and then is there a perfect blue sky with no clouds. In my life, there was hardly ever a perfect day, with no problems or clouds of sorrow.

The life inside our house was like a sky before a [violent] storm.

She didn't have any good feelings about herself anymore. Mom had broke her down to nothing. She stopped wearing her pretty blonde hair out, and she spent all of her time locked up in her room. Dad called her a bookworm who knew a lot of big words.

She had stopped trying to argue, even though Mom was always yelling at her. Sometimes she got pinched and slapped for nothing. A few times, I saw her start to cry, but she would just wipe her eyes and stop.

It had been building up for years. When it finally happened, it was worse than I could have imagined.

It was on a Saturday Morning. I remember it because Dad always worked on Saturday morning, and I was watching cartoons and eating cereal.

Another one of their arguments had started. I closed my door, so I wouldn't have to hear it. Sharon was in the bathroom, and they were yelling at each other through the door. After a while it stopped, and I thought it was over. But it started again, and it sounded like Mom was in the bathroom with her.

It suddenly got quiet. And then, I heard the loudest pop. Then I heard a loud [scuffling]. I put my cereal down and opened the door, then everything turned into slow motion.

That popping noise must have been a loud slap, because I saw them fighting. Sharon was in her underwear. They scared me so bad I almost closed the door. Mom was pulling Sharon's hair and pounding her on the head with her fist.

But Sharon's face was calm. She stopped fighting and pulled away.

Then she grabbed Mom's hair, and started hitting her in the face. Mom's voice made a weird sound. But she wasn't afraid. She tried to pull Sharon to the floor, but they kept slamming against the walls. They knocked the telephone table over, and a picture fell off the wall.

I think Sharon was holding back.

She grabbed Mom around the head, punching her so hard that I could hear it. Mom was trying to pull Sharon's bra off, and was yelling curse words. Then she tried to pull Sharon's underwear down. They stumbled towards my room, and I closed the door. They slammed into it so hard it sounded like they were going to crash through it. Then, I heard them fall to the floor.

I didn't want to open the door, but I couldn't help it. I can't describe how I felt.

Sharon was on top of Mom. They had each other around the neck. She just kept hitting Mom on top of the head. Mom wasn't even trying to get up, and then I saw why.

Her teeth were [clamped] down on Sharon's chest. It must have hurt because Sharon bit Mom on the shoulder in return.

They stood up fast, and I saw the bite mark on her [breast]. They were both breathing hard. Sharon moved her hair out of her eyes, and I saw a glad look on her face. Mom's face was scratched. The top of her white slip was torn.

I thought Mom gave up because she walked away. Sharon was in the middle of the big den with her hands on her hips, breathing like a runner. There were healed scars all over her back.

My heart jumped when Sharon turned and ran to her room, because Mom was coming towards her with a knife. I wanted to call the police.

Sharon locked her door, and Mom just stood there. Breathing. When the door opened again, she stuck the knife in the room and tried to get inside. Then she screamed and tried to pull her arm out. Sharon must have bit her arm. Then Sharon pulled her into the bedroom out of sight.

I heard them breathing hard but they weren't moving. When I looked inside, Sharon's arms and legs were wrapped around Mom's body. Then

Sharon held her hair to the floor, and smacked her in the face in the same spot over and over again. Mom grunted and tried to squirm from under her.

"Do you give up? Do you give up!"

When Sharon punched her again, I couldn't look anymore. But I could hear them. I wanted her to give up so Sharon would stop.

Then Mom screamed like she had been burned with a hot iron. I thought Sharon had stabbed her. I went back, and saw Sharon laying on top of her, biting Mom on the chest. Then she held her hair to the floor again and just kept punching her in the face. She hit her so many times that Mom was grunting loud from the pain. Every time Sharon made her scream, it hurt my insides.

When Mom walked out of the room, I saw blood on her face and her slip. Sharon came out behind her. She followed right behind into Mom's bedroom, and closed and locked the door. After a few minutes, I heard Mom hollering the same way Sharon used to. Sharon never told me what she did to her.

I didn't talk to her for the rest of that day. But when Dad walked into the house, more trouble started. He was slamming on her door, trying to get in her room. It sounded like he was trying to break the door down.

Sharon said she would do it again, if they ever touched her.

$\mathcal{I}$ don't believe there has ever been an oldest child of siblings, who has not been tempted to crumble under the unique pressures, even if not to succumb to the horrific violence that happened between my mother and me. I hope I have been forgiven for trying, in the briefest instant, to force a crossing over into the horrors of matricide. For a brief moment, I wanted to kill her.

For every bruise, for every welt, and for every drop of blood, I beat her. I endeavored to ruin her flesh in the heat of passion and revenge. I tried to punish her for each of the seventeen years of fear, dread and pain. With all of my strength, I attempted to bludgeon what beauty there was from her face, the way she had battered innocence from my body and soul.

Truly, there was no love lost between my mother and me that day, because there had been none left for either of us to give. Blood burning contempt had been fueled by the heat of her violence and perversion, until it blossomed into a fire of hatred.

This hatred was agitated, until it exploded into an inferno of murderous rage. I remember vividly, that it was a conscious thought that kept me from using that same knife, in the like manner she had intended for me. Even now, the weight of memories still burdens me, inciting me to inner rage, swirling into a tempest of issues that can never be fully unraveled and resolved.

But the unresolved past always reappears. It haunts the present like a phantom, obstructing the path towards peace of mind. Even now, I'm severely tormented by days long gone.

For Sarah, I maintained my bravest front on that rainy day in July. I had known for months that I would never be able to move with my family. I knew it was an infinite impossibility. For many weeks, I had allowed my sister to believe I was going with her.

I thank God that I found the nerve to tell her when I did.

November 27ᵗʰ

Winter will arrive early this year.

Mom locked the door again when she went out. For a split second, I thought maybe she wasn't going to lock it. She gave me steak for dinner. I think it was from a restaurant.

I think I was glad we were moving. There was too much misery on Sycamore Avenue.

Sharon started talking to me again after a while. She told me she was sorry for the way she acted. Summer was coming, and she was almost finished with her 11th grade year.

The worst time of my life began this June, on her last day of school. She took me for a long walk, all the way back to our old neighborhood. We went into the store we used to go to all the time. It had been two years since we had gone.

I felt very proud walking with Sharon. She was my beautiful sister, and my protector.

The lady in the store came from around the counter and hugged both of us. She kept talking about how tall and beautiful Sharon was, and she said I looked so different that she didn't recognize me. Sharon bought us Now & Laters in every flavor. Then we both got an orange [creamsicle], and ate them on the way home.

When we were walking home, she kissed me on the cheek, right in front of all the traffic. Her lips were cold. It didn't seem strange to me then, because she hugged and kissed me all the time.

When Mom and Dad left that night, Sharon came to my room and turned off my TV. There was a sad look on her face. She sat down on my bed, and told me to stand up in front of her. She looked at me for so long that I asked what was the matter.

"I can't go," she said.

My heart dropped, because I knew what she was talking about.

"Did Mom say you couldn't come with us?"

"I have to stay here and finish school. I'm going to live with Aunt Rose."

"Can I live there too?"

She looked at me like she was trying not to cry.

"I couldn't get them to let you stay."

The tears went to my throat when she said it. Then, they just came out of me.

"You'll be alright," [she said]. "You don't need me anymore."

"Why don't you want to stay with me?"

"I want to stay with you forever. But you know I can't live with them anymore."

I kept crying in her arms. I cried as hard as I could. I was hoping she would change her mind.

"They're going to punish me every day."

"No they won't," she said. "I was the one they punished all the time, not you. I'm going to call you every day when you get there. And I'll write you a letter every week. I promise."

Then she whispered softly in my ear.

"Don't be afraid. They need you to help them be happy. That's why they can't leave you. Because they love you."

I had begged her to come to Rocky Mount with us for just a few days. But she wouldn't do it. All of our stuff was already moved into the house. This house. Sharon and me had never even seen it before. We spent a lot of time with Aunt Rose in those last days.

Things had changed after the fight. I don't think Mom wanted her to live with us anymore. But Sharon swore she was going to stay with me every second until I left.

She threw away all of her old long dresses and skirts. Aunt Rose had took her shopping, and she had lots of new blouses and shoes. She had a lot of different kinds of pants and nice skirts and dresses. She said she didn't know why God invented bell bottom pants, and she swore she wouldn't ever buy any, even though Aunt Rose begged her to wear them. Aunt Rose had even bought her a little pair of diamond earrings. She wore them to her [Baptist] church the last Sunday we were there.

On the last day, she wore a pair of new blue jeans, a [sky] blue blouse, and a pair of black boots. I told her to tuck the pants inside the boots, but she wouldn't.

Sharon and me were in our empty living room. She had her arm around me, and we were looking at the rain outside the window. It was summer, but the day was chilly. She wore a long black raincoat. Her eyes were the color of spring. Her blonde hair was brushed long.

"Its time to go you two."

Except for the storm, it was quiet in the car. Sharon had put her arms around me and laid my head against her chest.

I didn't feel sad about leaving Sycamore Avenue. There was only pain in that house. All four of us were in the car together for the first time in months. It was miserable.

The ride to Aunt Rose's house was too short. We were in her driveway before I knew it. Mom and Dad both got out and took her things out of the trunk. I know they did it because they didn't want to stay in the car with her.

Sharon told me she loved me and to take good care of myself, and that soon we would be together again. She hugged and kissed me for the last time, and then she stepped out into the rain.

I wanted to get out, but Mom and Dad had already told me not too. They said they were in a hurry because of the weather. Aunt Rose opened the back door and gave me a big hug. I remember wishing she was my mother. I wanted her to make Mom let me stay.

I saw them all hugging each other on the porch. Dad hugged Sharon for real. I could tell he didn't want to leave her. I didn't think Mom was going to hug her, but she did. They didn't look at each other, though. It was a short, friendly hug. She didn't even kiss her daughter goodbye. Mom's hug with Aunt Rose was longer. Aunt Rose kissed her on the cheek.

Aunt Rose stayed on the porch while we drove out of the yard. I remember seeing all of those pretty flowers. Sharon was in her black coat with her black umbrella. She walked all the way in the street to watch us leave.

My sister was a figure dressed in black, waving to me while we drove to the end of the road. I waved back, but I know that she couldn't see me.

A summer thunderstorm was over us as we drove away. Lightning flashed in the clouds, and the Earth was covered in a mist of rain.

On the morning of December 1ˢᵗ 1979, I was awakened from what had already been a troubled sleep. I had tossed and turned, walking the floor, reading, writing, doing anything to try and coax slumber. I had been feeling deathly strange for several days, and had begun to wonder, even fear, that what was plaguing my spirit might be some vague allusion to premonition. But foreshadows of what? This I did not know.

When the phone rang at 7:31 on that cold Saturday morning, a thousand chimes responded from within, rattling, shaking me to my foundation— making me draw an icy breath, as if rising from beneath a dark ocean surface. It was as though what my soul had been dreading for days had finally pierced the night veil, gripping hold of every part of me.

I tried not to listen to what Aunt Rose was going to say on the telephone. But then she drew in that same breath of terror, and I heard her voice begin to quiver, and I had already begun to shake my head no. I refused to allow Satan's truth into my mind, even as I listened to soft footsteps creep towards me from somewhere on the other side of Creation.

When she opened her mouth to speak to me, I allowed every particle of my angry denial and contemptuous guilt to slice into her, and I ordered her with Hell's power to never speak those words to me. To never say them in my presence.

My Aunt Rose is a sturdy woman, given to fits of natural bravery. She had no fear of me, as she held me and forced the truth down my screaming throat that my sister had died the night before. Although she died from injuries sustained in a brutal beating, my parents pled no contest to negligent homicide, with probation and a fine, and were found guilty of nothing. But from that horrible past, to the present, and far into the future, I know that she died because I left her. I have nothing now but hope, that this will help bring some relief to my aching soul, and at least the smallest bit of purpose to my sister's tragic memory.

I lived in the Hell that was my parents' home for seventeen years. My little Sarah, until she was twelve.

The End

Memoriam

Elegy

My sister was a kind and gentle soul, with a spirit of love and compassion. Her brown eyes sparkled with the innocence and wonder of childhood. Her young features displayed a quiet wisdom and profound understanding. Sarah was my fortress. The lamp which helped guide me through this valley of shadows.

My own selfish motives stifled my duties as her protector. I knew the entire time I was making plans to rest in my earthly paradise, that she was going to be plunged into unearthly torment. This realization had built up inside me, until it reached that so-called critical mass, when energy is *about to be released in quantities too implausible to be believed. The proverbial guilty conscious starts it all, then torments the body with warnings of sustained sorrow, leading to emotional meltdown and psychological devastation.*

But I am comforted the least little bit, knowing that the last she saw of me was her tower of strength—with a smile, and a reassurance in her soul that everything was going to be fine, and that we would soon be together again.

When the car turned away, she could not see me still standing in the rain, in the middle of the road underneath my umbrella, mourning, praying for forgiveness for my selfish whims of escape. She was no witness to my own rescue from madness by my beloved Aunt who touched me, shocking me back to reality on that rainy day—escorting me through numbness into my house of safety.

My sister was not aware of the suffering that gripped every part of my body. It doubled me over, ripping a scream from inside me. It happened because I had a premonition of her suffering, even though I knew I was powerless to save her from it. I begged Providence, in the horror of true commitment, to protect her. I begged Him, through tears and sweat, to please protect her from my father's wrath, and my mother's perversion.

I drank deeply from that same cup of Holiness poison I loathed. Fasting, reading no book except for the Bible. For those three days after she left I died and was buried, then was resurrected into the same grief and depression that still touches my soul to this day.

Sarah, forgive me for having abandoned you! For having escaped from wretched Evil, leaving you in the clutches of burning, the clawing of endless suffering!

My Sarah...through misery I now go alone. There is no hope. No rest for souls in pain, from tortures laid at my feet.

Rest, my beautiful Sarah...

Rest forever in peace, and the glory of Paradise.

The Key

Sarah wrote of a dream image she had, which I am grateful she found comfort in, believing it foreshadowed success for me. She saw me adorned in a long, black coat, getting into a beautiful limousine. I know now that her mind had fed her a glimpse of our bleak future. Me being a mourner clad in black, leaving the church after having viewed her body.

Fate granted me mercy two times quickly, both on the night of her burial. My spirit was allowed some relief when she visited my dreams, hugging me, assuring me that she was happier than she had ever been. When I awoke from this dream, I can say with certainty that briefly, I was happy.

But later that same night, another dream disturbed my sleep. Powerful, equally as vivid as the first, but mysterious in purpose and intention.

This image saw me walking the halls of my mother's home, looking for my sister's room—a room I had never seen, having never before been inside the house. I found what I believed to be the door of her bedroom, and pushed it open slowly, finding the inside in no way unusual, except for one curious exception...

In the corner was a small, inconsequential little desk, with nothing on it except the most beautiful writing quill that can be imagined. There was no ink bottle, and no holder for the quill, which was laying in a natural position, as if it had been tossed on the desk and forgotten. This dream disturbed me so much that I told it to my Aunt Rose, who laid uneasy confirmation, telling me she had dreamed that Sarah was sitting at her own kitchen table, "writing up a storm."

The day my sister was buried, we went to my mother's home. I pushed my way through her sea of fellow mourners with all restraint, needing more than anything to get to her room, to gather for myself whatever little letter she may have written to me. When I stepped out of the cold, cavernous hallway into her little bedroom, it was as though I were transported elsewhere, into a kind of waking dream. A predestined reality. In the corner was indeed a small reading desk. But there was nothing on it.

I don't know what made me do it. But something inexplicable overwhelmed me, striking me with an urge to scour every hidden corner of her bedroom. I searched, checked, combed and examined every drawer. Every pocket, every book, nook and cranny—even moving the dresser to look behind it. But I found nothing. So in frustrated disappointment, I set about collecting all of her belongings to take with me.

The task gripped me, and I relaxed. Absorbing the room's energy. Allowing myself to feel, to hope that her essence was drifting from the walls, and becoming a part of me. I mothered her in my thoughts as I cleared every toy, trinket and piece of clothing from her closet. Every stitch of linen from her bed, and every pencil, pen and sheet of paper from her desk. When I opened the drawers on the mirrored dresser for the last time, I was resigned to the fact that there was no letter, and our dreams had only meant she had longed to talk to us. So I am sure I did not make it happen, when I pulled the bottom drawer out so far that it slipped and fell noisily to the floor.

A yellow notebook—curiously lost underneath the bottom dresser drawer—held little fascination for me when I reached into the dust and picked it up.

I will never know whether Fate has been cruel or kind to me, allowing me to open her Golden Key, reading the first words of something that plunged me into a whirlwind of shock, and intrepid days of despair. But I did know that every one of her little words rang with the truth of ages, and I knew that somehow, in some way, my life could never be the same, and all of this tragic madness was meant to be.

But for a long time, I buried the journal deep. Using its misery to fuel my own ambitions. I was educated at some distant land. Lost somewhere between here and those famed Ivy Paths, eventually becoming a teacher like my mother and father. But so many times, while I listened to my

footsteps echo through the empty knowledge palaces, I realized that for me, they were only hallowed halls of impossible hopes and fractured dreams. Emanating unquenchable melancholy. Glistening unfathomable despair.

It may not be important at all what I studied or taught, or what group of young minds between grade and graduate school I have lectured. But the fire burned out in my heart, and the desire froze in me. So I left the noble profession, retreating into the arms of my beloved Aunt, who had always been such a comfort to both of us during those dark years. I have spent my days and evenings underpaid, under-employed and under-appreciated. Tossed from this job to that. Whirled about on currents of restlessness and fear of committal. Ignoring the fact that anytime I felt the least bit trapped, it was time for me to go elsewhere.

So like many others I go forth. Tossed on winds of chaos and bitter cold. A winter soul. Drifting. Searching in vain for where to rest. Finding nothing but places I have already been.

A winter soul. Lost forever…in a frozen sea of regret.

Sharon Iris

ABOUT THE AUTHOR

Jonathan Lovejoy is a graduate of the University of North Carolina at Greensboro, with a B.A. in Religious Studies, and a graduate of Liberty University with an M.A. in Theological Studies. Divorced after 24 years of marriage, he is a graduate of Grand Canyon University with a Master of Divinity. He currently lives in Mesa, Arizona.

For more info on the author's life and career, visit jonathanlovejoy.com